Why Can't We Live Together Like Civilized Human Beings?

Also by Maxine Kumin

Fiction

Through Dooms of Love
The Passions of Uxport
The Abduction
The Designated Heir

Poetry

Halfway
The Privilege
The Nightmare Factory
Up Country: Poems of New England
House, Bridge, Fountain, Gate
The Retrieval System
Our Ground Time Here Will Be Brief:
New and Selected Poems

WHY CAN'T WE LIVE TOGETHER LIKE CIVILIZED HUMAN BEINGS?

Stories by
Maxine Kumin

The Viking Press New York

LIBRARY OF CONGRESS CATALOGING IN PUBLICATION DATA
Kumin, Maxine, 1925–
Why can't we live together like civilized
human beings?
I. Title.
PS3521.U638W5   813'.54   81-69967
ISBN 0-670-76553-8   AACR2

Grateful acknowledgment is made to the following publications in which these stories first appeared, and for permission to reprint a selection from another source:

Ontario Review: "On This Short Day of Frost and Sun"; *The Paris Review:* "Another Form of Marriage"; *Penmaen Press, Ltd.:* "The Banquet," from *Banquet: Five Short Stories,* edited by Joan Norris; *Ploughshares:* "West"; *Quarterly West:* "The Perfect Body"; *The Real Paper:* "The Town Records Its Deaths"; *Redbook:* "These Gifts"; *Tri-Quarterly Review:* "The Missing Person" and "A Traveler's Hello"; *Virginia Quarterly Review:* "To Be of Use" and "The Neutral Love Object."

Viking Penguin Inc.: A selection from *Journey Around My Room: The Autobiography of Louise Bogan* by Ruth Limmer. Copyright © 1980 by Ruth Limmer, Trustee, Estate of Louise Bogan.

Printed in the United States of America
Set in Electra

*for Victor
and for Jane, Judith, Daniel
and for Yann*

How preposterous, how unbearable is literature: reality dished up in the phrase; men and women inflated out of recognition by the noun, verb, adverb, adjective. . . . The paper people in books, who have one agony to endure, *one* set of toils to fight clear of, in their lives. . . . —One should set oneself the task, in full maturity, to fix on paper the bizarre, disordered, ungainly, furtive, mixed elements in one's life, the opposite of the paper people—and the men and women in masks, halved queerly in their natures—the destiny which stands half in us, half about us, and is often in the hands of these split and equivocal beings. . . .

—Louise Bogan

Contents

Why Can't We Live Together Like Civilized Human Beings?

Another Form of Marriage

They were touring New England, escaped lovers in mid-June, when the signs sprang up, hand-lettered in red and green on shiny white boards. 5 MILES TO SKYVUE STRAW-BERRY FARM! the first one proclaimed, followed in due course by SKYVUE STRAWBERRY FARM 1 MILE ON LEFT and PICK YOUR OWN AT SKYVUE STRAWBERRY FARM 10 TO 4.

"Let's," she said, squeezing the brown corduroy of his knee.

"But what will we do with them?" he said, thinking of tonight's motel somewhere in the Champlain Valley and tomorrow's drive down the Hudson to their separate suburbs. He would leave her at the train station just as he had last year, and the year before, and the year before that. As if she had ridden the local out from Grand Central, she would take a taxi home.

"Eat them. Take them home. Oh, never mind!" she despaired. She had caught sight of herself at the taxi stand, strawberries spilling out of her shopping bags.

1

But he had downshifted from fourth to third and then, at the last declarative sign, STRAWBERRIES ARE RICH IN VITAMIN C, to second. They turned in at the driveway, rose up a winding dirt road, and were there.

They had come from the translation seminar held each summer at a small college in the Adirondacks. He specialized in Hungarian, which was not, however, his native tongue. Always from the bottom of his suitcase he took out the two volumes of his German-Hungarian dictionary. These stood on the bureau, on a succession of bureaus on stolen weekends throughout the year, grave necessary friends of their liaison. She spoke no foreign language, but served the conference as administrative assistant, cutting stencils each morning, collating pages of prose and poetry in bilingual arrangements. She saw to it that the original always appeared on the left-hand page so that the work under discussion might lie as flat as an open-face sandwich.

That first summer she had come to the conference unexpectedly, filling in for an ill colleague. She was a shyly attractive woman in her thirties, tallish and slender with long brown hair that she wore tucked discreetly into a knot at the nape of her neck. It was rainy and raw; she had not brought warm clothing and the man who was not yet her lover had loaned her a comforting maroon ski sweater in which, he assured her, she looked properly waif-like. It smelled of his brown tobacco cigarettes tinged with camphor. When he smiled, she was dazzled by one off-center gold tooth. She began wearing a pair of dangling imitation-gold earrings. He came to her room the fourth night, whistling nonchalantly up the stairs of the old brown building, a sheaf of papers in his hand. Raindrops had peppered his beret, and she propped it on the radiator to dry. But the papers were in Spanish, five versions of a Neruda poem left over from that morning's workshop, and out of his mackintosh pocket there came a bottle of cognac. At dawn, holding his shoes, he went lightly down the fire escape, onto which, luckily, one of her windows opened.

A highway bisected the campus. Porches of the college buildings overlooked it and words were often lost in the drift of traffic. Snatches came through: "Do you see this as an exercise?" "Do you set yourself models?" "The basic concept is very good, really very good. . . ." Logging trucks passed in both directions, confusing her. Those great prehistoric-looking tree trunks, stacked like her sons' Playskool toys, rattled past in their chains. Perhaps there were sawmills at either end of this mountain gap? The process of overlap struck her as an apt image for translation.

Skyvue Farm provided its own boxes: wax-lined cardboard trays, really, for picking. What he was to do with the damn things was another story. They could be given away, he supposed. Bartered against the motel bill, a hundred miles down the road? The view, or *vue*, if you will, was truly incredible. To the west, spruce- and pine-covered hills the color of bleached denim. East, looking into the determined sun of Vermont, three small connected ponds with ducks on them. And stretching its plateau in a commodious rectangle of what he took to be easily ten acres, this expanse of strawberry field, still swallowing up its odd assortment of human forms as people entered, were assigned their rows, and sank to their knees or buttocks. Some few more or less leaned down, rumps high, and dug their hands into the plants or rested one palm on the earth for equilibrium as they picked.

He was forty-five this year; his life was flawed and sedentary, he groaned, folding himself down. The berries adorned the plants tritely. He resented the dew that added diamonds to their rubies. How monstrous the fruit were, the ripest ones leaving behind a little white cone on the plant as they pulled away from the calyx. In Austria

3

the strawberries grew elusively in the meadows, and he was forced out into the fields each morning with the other young ones to crawl through prickly grasses and fill his pail. Mosquitoes sang in his ear. His mother would fly into a rage if he scanted on the picking. Once, invoking his father at the Front, she beat him with a shoe. Those wild strawberries, he remembered, were long and cylindrical and hung from the creeping vine like sows' teats. He tasted salt and wondered if he had been crying. No, it was sweat. Or did it matter? He mopped his face with a handkerchief and sat down between rows. Memory was exhausting in full sun.

Often there had been no bread in the bakery and no flour in the house to bake with. Now, whipped cream rose up in mountains on his strawberry shortcake. Now he had a wife and half-grown children, the oldest to enter college that fall. And in the mountains, a mistress—dreadful old-fashioned word! What was he but an old-fashioned, fastidious middle-aged linguist?—a mistress only slightly younger than his wife and a history, going on four years now, of stolen weekends. It came to him that he had pretended more translations than he had effected. Each one sweetened the months of fidelity that followed.

It was a hot morning and promised to be a hotter day. She had picked well past him, turned, and had started greedily back still another row so that now she was coming toward him in a series of little frog hops. He saw her thighs flash white, and her fingers pinching here, there, so decisively nipping the best berries; yes, he would nip and pinch and comfort and take hold. Now she was closer, now clearly he could see the gray streaks she lamented were overtaking her hair. How luminous, that chestnut mane, against the sun! Their quarrels were sharper each year, their reconciliations almost unbearably poignant. His wife was paler, larger, a milder version. Against his will he remembered the rented summer cottage at the shore when

4

the children were small, how his wife served him berries
with cream for a late-night snack, moving furtively about
the unfamiliar kitchen, whispering over his bowl. He could
hear the click of his spoon on the crockery and knew after-
wards exactly how they had bedded, he stroking the back
of her neck first. Oh, he was a detestable person; he de-
served neither woman, he told himself, even knowing the
thought was an act of self-congratulation.

Meanwhile in the strawberry patch he was sentenced to
overhear just behind him a tale of loyalty, of a man stand-
ing by his wife struck down by multiple sclerosis or cancer,
he could not tell from the medical details. In any case,
incapacitated, her condition unchanging. Two women, lo-
cal, he guessed from their accents, harvesting berries for
their freezers, jellies, pies, were exchanging the details
of this story. She had fainted on the commode, she spat
blood, he still took her on fine days for drives, tucking her
wasted body about with pillows. Only in Purgatory was
one doomed to hear such tales of domestic heroism.

Now the woman who was not his wife had drawn
abreast of him and saw from the passivity of his shoulders
that she was making him unhappy. In that buddha pose
she would have kissed the worry lines from the corners
of his mouth. Instead, displaying the half-filled box, she
begged, "Just five minutes more." He smiled evasively, a
cocktail party smile of dismissal, and moved forward in his
row. They squatted there, back to back, her fingers travel-
ing expertly over the plants while she reflected on their
stolen weekends.

She could name them all sequentially, passing quickly
over the rainy one in Indiana where they had fished in the
St. Jo River full of disgusting carp and then drunk them-
selves into a sodden state in the one downtown hotel. He
had pushed her beyond her limits; dark anger had flowed
out of her like blood clots, and passion, equally ungov-
erned, rushed in. Never in her other life had she been an

5

extremist. Now she recorded impressions with her stomach, her skin. The mind came last of all in this procession. It had begun with the glint of gold in the mouth of an elegant foreign man, but where would it end? She could recall especially the grit and detritus of New York City, where they met often, the enforced gaiety of its bars gleaming metal and dark at noon. Once there had been dinner at the Russian Tea Room, where an old man at the next table, knowing them for conspirators, palpably, lovingly, fondled them with glances. He and the translator had conversed in German.

Out of town she remembered there were chains of look-alike motels where air conditioners exhaled noisy droplets and overhead fans started up in windowless bathrooms at the flick of a light switch. The toilets wore Good Housekeeping seals of paper bands. She swore and paced the corridors while he was gone or else sat for hours in a hot tub as if hoping her skin, that pimple, would burst.

She bit into a deformed strawberry swollen almost to plum size. It was mealy but wet as the earth was wet to her fingers, as the plants were furry with their cultivated bristles. Spiders clambered up the wisps of straw that had been spread as mulch between rows and spun and fell and labored again to renew their torn webs.

Bits of conversation drifted down her row. Even here, the talk was of ungrateful teen-age children, of dying parents, sick animals. She felt a dull astonishment. In this whole Brueghel scene of people bending, kneeling, plucking, in this landscape of bobbing colors and anatomies, a terrible banal sameness prevailed. It was the sameness of the human condition. She had come to put her hands into the dirt, to taste her fruit in the full sun. For even in these carefully tended furrows to which the pickers were directed by the farmer's sharp-faced wife dressed in her strawberry-dotted pinafore, even though the hybrid berries had been force-fed to this size and drenched, midway in

6

their span, with insecticides, they were more real than their counterparts in supermarket boxes, plasticked over and fastened shut with rubber bands.

Her legs and back ached. She had come impulsively, she now saw, licking the strawberry juice from her fingers, to put the wildness back in this dear red fruit. At the expense of the man she adored, who was fluent in five languages and whose starved childhood had been stained with this sort of foraging.

What was this affair but another form of marriage? Instead of being faithful to one man, she was faithful to two. Her husband was industrious and kindly and a bit unkempt. She remembered she had loved his ragged beard, his abandon with clothing, the way he wore his pipe, still smoldering, in his back pocket. When his shoestrings broke, he knotted them. When she closed her eyes she saw him, young and laughing, his arms full of their two boys, a tangle of hair and beard and arms and legs. The red dots of strawberries behind her eyes brought back that time, ten years gone, her standing stirring at the stove, him slicing bread, the little ones leaning on their elbows at the table waiting to taste the hot jam. "Will it jell?" they had asked, using their new word. "Will it ever jell?"

Everything jelled, filled its spaces or found new spaces to flow into. Thus she had come, willy-nilly, to adore a tidy professor whose suitcase was meticulously packed, his shaving lotion in a plastic bottle, his shirts in see-through bags fresh from the laundry, a man who carried his dictionaries about with him like religious statuary.

She rose, dusted herself off, and together the lovers, each encumbered with a tray, stood in line to have the fruit weighed. "Boxes or bags?" the pinafore woman asked impatiently. It came to ten pounds' worth, two brown bags full, which they set on the floor of the back seat and covered with the *New York Times* as the coolest place in the car.

All that day and the next the berries ripened and ran together in their twin bags, giving off a smell of humus and fermented sugar. All that day and the next, winding their way downstate from Mecca, the guilty pilgrims breathed in that winey richness and did not speak of it. In the twilight of the last twenty miles along the Taconic State Parkway they sat very close, she with her left hand sorrowfully on his knee, he with his right hand nuzzling hers in her lap. At the last rest area before the turnoff to her suburb he swerved wordlessly, pulled up to a green trash barrel, and stopped the car. "Yes," she said. "I know," she said. And he divested them both of the bloody evidence. Then he took her to her train station and, kissing her goodbye, drove his tongue between her teeth like a harsh strawberry and she clung to him, this other man, this vine which had taken root and on which she ripened.

The Facts of Life

Y our heart beats hard when you run, but not when you're dead," says one little flat-faced girl, my youngest child with the surprising cheekbones. She is poking the remains of a beached fish. "Your guts fall out when you're dead."

"You have guts too," her older sister warns. "Just like the animals."

The children are making gritty sandballs on our backyard strip of Puget Sound. The sand of the Olympic Peninsula is coarse and new, with an admixture of clay. The girls carry these rudimentary round things out on the pier and with ceremony drop them in the frothing ocean.

"This is the fetus of Annabelle. Down goes Annabelle. Goodbye, Annabelle!" they chant, and return to the beach to take up their work under a late August sun.

The repellent name of this game is Abortion. I have no idea when they garnered this notion. They have been playing it for three weeks while my mother shrinks day by day a mile inland in St. Agnes Hospital. The schedule is this: I go to the hospital mornings, after doctors' rounds, and sit by my mother's bed for an hour watching her inhale oxygen through a plastic tube taped to her left nostril. Afternoons, I go with the kids to the beach. In the evenings my husband and I return to the hospital to look in on Mama. I check for bedsores; I survey as dispassionately as an administrator the appurtenances of the trade: I.V. stand, urine bag, oxygen tank, African violet plant on the dresser. The patient is comatose, the condition irreversible. On the chart at the foot of the bed, discreetly: DNR. Do not Resuscitate.

We have lived in the Pacific Northwest for ten years now. My mother has been with us the last two of these. Although everyone in her family dies young of congestive heart failure—only one of her nine siblings survives—I have clung all summer to the notion that Mama will outlast this episode. This week it becomes evident that she is dying. Her youngest brother, Steve, the one she virtually raised after her own mother, worn out with childbearing, took to bed with her phlebitic legs, is flying toward us from New York. Even as the fetus of Harriet follows those of Mary Anne and Donna into the shockingly cold seawater, Uncle Steve is in the air over the Midwest hurtling toward us.

I look at my almost-twelve-year-old daughter, the curly-haired one with a saddle of freckles across her nose. Her body is leaving behind the simple peanut-shell shape I have grown so accustomed to. The outlines of energetic little breasts emerge. Hair has begun to shade the porcelain mons. Any day now she will start to menstruate. She is longing to begin. She and her friends will hire a hall complete with brass band to announce it, says my husband. They'll light a victory bonfire and dance around it all night in their baby-doll pajamas; they'll smear their foreheads with indigo and run wild among the beech trees.

He is right, of course. The telephone network is waiting.

An eager band of little girls, itchy with the work of sprouting, sits expectant. The old reticences, embarrassments, and complaints have given way to progress. Now we have sex education, cartoon films of the reproductive tract, a beltless sanitary napkin, a slender, virginal tampon. We say we are armed and ready, Olympian and detached, but the truth is we huddle here, terrified parents.

When I was an only and late child in Baltimore, my mother took in unwed mothers. It was wartime; pregnancy was epidemic. Because she was on the Board of Directors of the Honeycott Home for Wayward Girls and had a musical talent, my mother took on the special cases. Special cases expressed a burning desire to play the piano. Sometimes they had a real gift. They wore handmade blue smocks over kangaroo skirts with a cutout pouch for enlarging into. The suitcases they carried were always cardboard, the fake leather design already peeling from the corners.

The unwed mothers lived, serially, in a mean little dormered room on the third floor. They were treated not quite like servants, nor yet like family. Sociology had only recently been invented; it was difficult to know how to fit them in. When they first came up the herringbone-brick walk, under the white Ionic pillars, through the glassed-in vestibule of tentacled rubber plants, they seemed sullen. What had they done to be thrust into this mansion on Poplar Hill?

D E F—tuck the thumb—G A B C D! my mother instructed tirelessly, back ramrod stiff at the Steinway baby grand. After scales ran the arpeggios, followed by Czerny exercises with the best fingerings penciled in over the notes. All afternoon the double parlor doors held in grace notes and chords and fragments of Clementi or Couperin. Sometimes I sat outside in the square front hall and watched dustings of sun motes vibrate to the tympany of the piano. Tone-deaf, I was spared my mother's rigor.

11

When the music stopped and the doors grated open, Minna or Jackie would emerge, minuets and gypsy airs in hand. Little round belly pressed against the blue smock, sweat beading her upper lip, in her eye the wild look of a just-uncaged bird. Would it be better to endure disgrace in Rehoboth or Harkers Corners than this bludgeoning of daily lessons?

"They haven't had your advantages," my mother said. "They haven't had a lovely big bedroom of their own and a white organdy spread and a dressing table." These were all things I detested, pawns in the war we waged on one another. My sneakered feet left imprints on the spread. Drawings of horses, bits and pieces of games, apple cores littered the dressing table. Sweaters turned inside out, sneakers, and the beloved white bobby sox spilled out of the closet.

The unwed mother I remember best was Estrella Jean, a large fair-haired girl whose family ran a truck farm near the Delaware Water Gap. From the time she was big enough to toddle down the rows, Estrella Jean spent her summers picking cucumber beetles off the vines, into a jar of kerosene. She pinched back tomato suckers and hilled the potatoes. When she was fifteen she ran away from home before the squash vines had set their second leaves. "It got so all I could think about was those beetles, the way they wiggle off your fingers waving around till they drop. I couldn't do it another minute. I just packed up my Sunday dress and five dollars and hitched my way outa there."

Estrella Jean never talked to anyone but me about the soldier she loved. The Honeycott people did not even know his name, which was Dwayne Root, and if I ever told, Estrella Jean promised she would cut my tongue out of my mouth with my mother's fish knife.

"But I never would! Not if they torture me," I protested.

"You don't know what you'd do if they tortured you. A person is not responsible under torture."

I thought about this. I was ten, in a ruffled bedroom in Baltimore. Nazis tortured the Jews. They also tortured the Allies and spies dropped behind the lines. "I'd scream but I wouldn't tell. I'd pass out."

Estrella Jean was trying a new hair style from *McCall's* magazine. "Never mind that shit. You can't pass out just from wanting to. Read me what you do next."

" 'Section the hair in layers,' " I read obligingly. " 'Then, starting with the top layer, wet the hair with setting lotion and roll under as for a page boy. Turn the roll toward your face and secure with two clips.' "

"Anyway, if they torture you it's all right to tell," she amended.

"When Dwayne comes back, will you marry him?"

"When he comes back he'll go with me and we'll find our baby, wherever the Honeycotts have placed it, and then we'll go back that night and sneak in and take it away." This was one variation in the ongoing fantasy Estrella Jean and I built.

My mother was vague on the subject of pregnancy out of wedlock; that was what she called it in formal conversation. The unwed moms had not had my advantages, advantages which presumably would keep me from becoming one of them. They desperately wanted their babies. They fought to be allowed to keep them. Wiser, more mature, educated people in charge of the disposition of newborns would not permit them even to see the infants they had carried. It was kinder. An unwed mother was not told the sex of her child. She had the assurance that it was well cared for, that it went to a loving, financially secure, and childless couple—a couple pictured as grieving over their barren state. The unwed mom was urged to return to her community, pick up the tatters of her former life, and carry on, a sober, disciplined person, able to take charge of her feelings, for hadn't all counseling encouraged this self-knowledge?

The baby is a love object for these young girls, parroted my mother. Many of them were battered about in their childhood, sixty percent come from families where alcohol is a problem, she recited. Our own whiskey was kept locked away in the cabinet. Our own family feelings were carefully controlled in the presence of the moms. We were unfailingly polite and cheerful.

All her life Estrella Jean had loved music. She loved to dance and sing, she wrote little tunes in her head and held them there, for she had not yet learned to write music and could not set them down. Now, in her own musical notation book, she copied out a melody a night and sometimes sneaked back downstairs after everyone had gone to bed to test its harmony and charm on the piano. She was working on lyrics for some of the melodies; I was privileged to supply her with rhyme words which flew into my head like thoughtless sparrows. Probably our second-most popular fantasy was the one in which a record company discovered Estrella Jean and she was catapulted overnight into stardom. Modestly I skulked in the background. Perhaps I would run away with her and Dwayne Root and the baby to a Spanish-style villa in the Hollywood Hills.

During Estrella Jean's tenure, one of my girl cousins and I brashly agreed to a game of Doctor with visiting boy cousins a few years older. I remember that we swathed our heads in bath towels in the naive belief that if we covered our faces the boys would not be able to tell us apart. But when it was their turn to enter the examining room, they arrived, after much whispering and snickering, in their underpants and would proceed no further. Nothing to see but strange, shifting bulges, as if each boy had a captive mouse behind his Cloroxed white fly.

Later, fully clothed but obviously aroused, we played

Spin the Bottle. "If you let a boy put his tongue in your mouth he can make you do anything," Alice admonished me.

Nevertheless, it happened.

Visions of sperm leaping out of his tongue and slithering down my throat tormented me. I could not eat. Every mouthful I swallowed fell on top of the fishlike baby already growing in my belly. Finally, unable to go on with this enormous duplicity, I told not my mother but Estrella Jean.

"Where you been all your life, Leah Anne? You are dumber than a peahen," she said, astonished.

But when she told me the stuff they do on top of you, I tried not to believe her. "Why would anyone want?"

"You'll find out, little Miss Priss," was all Estrella Jean would say.

Not long after, the blessed event took place. I remember hearing a good deal of bustling about in the night. Doors opened and closed, the brake of the Packard unstitched, the motor turned over, but I never came fully awake.

"She had a bad time of it and no wonder," my mother was saying to my father the next morning at breakfast. "Nine pounds, seven ounces."

He clucked, shaking his head in sympathy.

"And café au lait."

My father murmured something conciliatory and was gone for the day.

I found out soon enough what they had been talking about. Because it was the wrong color, Estrella Jean was permitted to keep her infant. I, who understood nothing of the logistics of baby farming, rejoiced secretly.

I saw Estrella Jean twice more. The first time, a fat caramel buddha in her arms, she came to collect her clothes and her music. Lucky, lucky Estrella Jean with a live and gurgling baby doll to hold! Any day now Dwayne

15

Root would reappear and make an honest woman of her. Then the baby would have a father and they could begin to live happily ever after.

The second time, a year or so later, I crouched out of sight at the top of the stairs as a desperate Estrella Jean begged to be allowed to come back to Poplar Hill to live—"just for a little while, just till I can get a job and a place of my own"—and was turned away. Sorrowfully, tenderly, with a twenty-dollar bill and good advice and a prepaid taxi downtown, but rejected as definitively as if she had proposed arson or embezzlement.

After the taxi pulled away, I flung into the set piece, weeping.

Scrooge! I cried against my father. I called my mother a mean bitch. How could they? Why? I demanded.

That kind of language was precisely why. For my own good, I was told. Impressionable age, bad influence, and so on. Estrella Jean was damned so that I might be saved. Meanwhile I ranted that I was not worthy.

Clearly it was time to educate me. I was given two books: *Growing Up: How You Became Alive, Were Born, and Grew,* by Karl de Schweinitz, of which most memorably there comes back a page bare of all decoration except for a pure black dot at the center. The text informed me that once I was smaller, even, than that dot. Little was said about the mechanics of conception. Perhaps a very bright child could deduce from the euphemisms about loving one another very much exactly how the father's penis made its way into the mother's vagina. Perhaps the text was sufficiently graphic, but I was not ready to visualize this bizarre event.

The other book, a mere pamphlet really, was entitled *Marjorie May's Twelfth Birthday* and addressed itself in exalted language to the even more mysterious subject of menstruation. It would happen when I was twelve, that much was apparent. But somehow I inferred—or needed to infer—that this catastrophic series of events would take place only during my twelfth year. With patience and fortitude I could outlast the ugly visitation. By age thirteen it would be over with, and I could resume my rightful post as center on the local scrub football team.

On the face of it, the etiquette of sex information and the etiquette of dying have little in common. In truth the same prurience, the same resentments obtain in both. Did I want the unvarnished truth? No more than my mother, gathering up the frail skirts of her dignity, wanted it then or now. She intends to sweep into heaven on her legacy of station in the life just past. She does not acknowledge the facts of life, the fact of death.

Until the twilight state of coma closed them down, the vitality in my mother's face concentrated in her eyes. Even in age the blue irises did not pale or go runny, but deepened like a northern lake. Still she brightened her lips with a savage red tube. She wore a blue rinse on her hair, which lay in orderly finger waves against her scalp, the pink skin like pale ribbons shining between the waves.

All my life I watched that face on guard against invasion. Something mysterious held my mother in check. Intimacy offended her. How gross I was, with my raw feelings! Always too happy or too sad, too hungry or replete, despairing of that gentility, that self-control my mother cherished. I looked and behaved so little like her that it seemed entirely possible I was a changeling child. A mistake had been made in the nursery of Johns Hopkins Hospital.

This final year of her life with me, my mother repeats all the old stories that have worn a groove in her mind. It is like a needle left to play, generations later, the hit tunes from *My Fair Lady*. I hear again and again the small story of her early career, darkly daring against her father's wishes, as piano accompanist to a violinist. I see my father coming onstage at a party, late; I see him framed in the

17

doorway as she plays a Chopin sonata, lounging there, an insolent stranger. Six months later, on her thirty-first birthday, despite all family and parish pressures, she elopes with him. Out of the faith, out of the close constraining nest, I see my small mother fly into my father's arms.

Was it a happy marriage? It was a secretive one. My parents had separate rooms. If my father had anything to say to my mother—at least while I was within earshot on the second floor—he came to her door and knocked for admittance. I remember my shock the first time I saw a double bed in a playmate's parents' bedroom. "But where does your father sleep?" I asked. In that house on Poplar Hill, lonely and singular, I heard over and over that I was a *wanted* child. *Planned,* my mother stressed, who had grown up in the middle of a big, boisterous crop of siblings, having to see to her little brothers herself as annual pregnancy brought her mother low.

Grizzled Uncle Steve, the family baby, arrives in a taxi from the airport. He dazzles us all in his black turtleneck and red corduroy pants. We eat a cold, patchy supper and hurry to St. Agnes'.

"Polly, Polly, listen!" he says to the little body in the bed. "Polly, it's your Stevie boy come home, come home to his other mama."

Do her eyelids flutter? The nurse shakes her head.

"All of you, clear out now," Steve says. "People hear what you say to them, even in coma. I want to talk to my Poll."

Whatever he tells her, if she hears him, she can let go now, and does. At noon the next day she slips quietly out. Subliminally, maybe she has been waiting to say goodbye to this truly first child of hers, unwanted and unplanned.

We decide not to have a public funeral. After the body is cremated we go, my daughters, my husband, my uncle, and I, to scatter her ashes on the beach below the house. The phrase for this is: in accordance with her wishes. It is the beach on which her grandchildren play their inventive modern games.

That night over double scotches I ask Steve what he said to Mama. More than what to say to nubile daughters, I need to learn how to talk to the dying.

He shakes his head, like a lawyer or psychiatrist. It is privileged information. Instead, he tells me this story.

When my mother was a young girl she was taken to Europe by her one wealthy spinster aunt. The crossing was rough; they docked at Le Havre and set out immediately for the Golden City of Paris. There my mother was abducted and used—the word is Uncle Steve's—by a middle-aged banker to whom Aunt Elsa had a letter of introduction. Three days later, by convincing him that she cared for him and would return, my mother broke away. That was all she ever saw of the Continent. Six weeks later she had a therapeutic abortion in New York City. She was Estrella Jean's age.

I try to imagine this encounter and fail utterly. I try to believe that it happened. I want to let it account for so much, for the Victorian prudishness, for the whole Honeycott adventure, for the polite but yawning distance between my parents. Their pellmell romance, the reckless elopement seem now more plausible.

Two weeks later my daughter's first blood comes. She is terribly happy, terribly sad; terribly hungry, overstuffed. Women together, we try to keep the celebration down to a dull roar.

The Neutral Love Object

On the way over to the Island they composed the kind of grouping commonly sought by fashion photographers. One of those faintly insolent, terribly insouciant family sets you see from time to time in *Vogue* magazine, Sue Swanson thought. The still-youthful mother and father, athletic and well-nourished; the married daughter who improves on them both in profile, with the wind lifting and tunneling through her long brown hair; the European son-in-law with his brief beard and ever so slightly down-turning mustache. And of course the dog, the obligatory panting golden retriever obediently sprawled at his master's feet. The difference being, she noted silently, that we are pretenders in this glossy, and our golden is one-half ancestry unknown.

A few other late vacationers lounged at the rail, lifting already tanned faces to the September sun, but they had the top deck of the ferry pretty much to themselves. After the *Cranston* had delivered its three right-of-way hoots and the ship had settled into a vigorous bobbing motion, Sue began unpacking the picnic basket Bertrand had carried up from the station wagon parked in its allotted slot below. Ham and cheese sandwiches for Douglas, her husband, and for Bertrand, her son-in-law, Bertrand's with Dijon mustard. For Cindy and herself, the penitential yogurt. Potato chips for the men. Carrot sticks for the women. For the men, chocolate cupcakes. Apples for all. Biscuits for Agamemnon, who had been denied breakfast as a precaution against seasickness. He dispensed with these in one gluttonous swipe and waited slavishly for the sandwich crusts and cake crumbs that were also his birthright.

Once at a cocktail party a psychiatrist had told her that people make their dogs into neutral love objects, a repository for all the unspoken passion at work in the yeasty ferment of a family. And she had smiled passively, agreeing with him. So they had. They were furthermore, the kind of family that gives its animals royal, heroic, mythological names. There had been Castor and Pollux, Cindy's dapple-gray ponies; Oedipus and Caesar, Peter's pygmy goats of one summer. Melissa's cat had been named Cleopatra, her one surviving kitten, Cassandra. And, in this case, fourteen years of Agamemnon, who had as a puppy slept in one child's bed after another, transported from place to place with his wind-up clock wrapped in a towel, his teddy bear, and his teething bone. Cindy had been eight, Melissa six, and Peter four when he came into their world. The trouble was, he would not live long enough. The trouble with love was, it could be outlasted.

Someone else's apricot poodle was loose on deck. Two children bounded after it, their matching suede jackets flapping. They called Heather, Heather! in angry little bursts. The dog was finally cornered piddling on an exhaust vent and borne away as it yipped piteously.

"Someone ought to put the laisse to them," Bertrand remarked.

"Leash," Cindy said. "*On* them."

It was the fifth correction of the day, Sue thought. But why am I counting? I suppose he's just as hard on her French. And then the Thurber cartoon came into her head: When did the magic go out of our marriage?

But the sun was soothing, the illusion of open sea restful. She dozed finally, tipped back in one chair, her feet braced on another, the thrum of the engines jarring her cheekbones, and woke with a mild headache.

"There's Gardiner's Light," Douglas called from the rail. His hair blew forward from the crown, revealing a developing bald spot. "That's where you throw a penny overboard if you want to come back."

"On the way over?" Cindy was doubtful. "I thought only on the way back." Her tone said plainly, *If you've had a good time.*

"On the way back seems logical," Sue said. And then, for no reason, "I love islands."

Douglas came over and put his arm around her. "The mind is an island."

"Yours, maybe," she told him. "Mine is nothing but a cranberry bog at this point."

They were all so tired, after what was to have been a joyous summer. For Bertie had gotten his agrégation and Cindy had finished her provisional year teaching and they had agreed to forsake Geneva, beautiful in that season, to spend the summer in Boston. And then the phone call: Cindy, ashen calm, coming to find her in the garden squatting in the carrot row. *Now, Mother, sit down a minute? Goggy fell down a flight of stairs and broke her hip? In Lake Forest? It's her next-door neighbor, a somebody Ashendon?*

Weekly flights to Chicago ensued. Her mother appeared to be cheerfully mending in a convalescent home. Sue brought her potted plants, needlework, magazines, pictures of the grandchildren. And then pneumonia. The double anniversary party—their twenty-fifth, Cindy and Bertie's first—hastily called off. Bleak hours in the hospital, waiting to be allowed the thirty-minute visit. Bleaker ones in between in the airport. A stroke. Specialists. Dozens of telephone calls recklessly placed person-to-person at the peak hours. And finally, grudgingly, mercifully, death entered, imposing more responsibilities. Meanwhile, in Boston, Cindy bought Peter a suit for the funeral. Melissa came back from her American Friends' sponsored summer on an Indian reservation. Bertie slept in her mother's vacant house until Douglas, who had been in Panama supervising the installation of a power line, returned. Coward that she was, she would not stay in her childhood bedroom without him. Too many ghosts, was all she said.

"Everybody's mother has to die sometime," Melissa said, meaning to be reasonable. "In the Navaho culture they *celebrate* the deaths of the parents. They *rejoice* that their spirits have gone to join the ancestors."

"Lissa," Peter said, fingering his new haircut. "Do me a favor. Take a deep breath, okay? Now see how long you can hold it."

And then the house was put on the market and Bertie and Peter, during a record heat wave, hauled away all the detritus of her mother's long widowhood.

She grieved as quietly as possible. She had been an only child, a late arrival, and she was only ten when her father died. Her mother took over his real estate office and drew a vital energy from it. It was as if she had saved something of him by keeping his business alive. She had never encouraged intimacy between mother and daughter, and they lived side by side inside their baggy sweaters with the thermostat set low. Explaining to Douglas, trying to keep the tears out of her voice, Sue said, "It was serene. Chilly, but serene. I never questioned it."

Now she thought, *But I left too soon.*

The stresses had opened little cracks in everyone. Not the least in Agamemnon, who had been kenneled for three days and had neither eaten nor drunk water the entire time. "You should have started when he was very young," the vet said reproachfully. Now Melissa had returned to Oberlin with her sand paintings, Peter with his duffelbag and guitar had entered Reed, and the last four of them were on their way—"Look! there it is!" Sue said—to the magical island where they had never been.

The harbor town was determinedly quaint. An absence of gaudy storefronts, no billboards, gas lamps on the still-cobbled main street. The shingled houses, uniformly unpainted, weathered to a silvery gray. Fat and disdainful seagulls sat on pilings or followed the lobster boats in and out of port. And everywhere an air of restraint, of self-sufficiency, Yankee pride or pluck. Bertrand was enchanted; it could have been Denmark, or the Frisian Islands. "It's so . . . un-American!" he congratulated.

The weather, miraculously, held. They were in the midst of a Bermuda high with spectacular sunsets and only thinly foggy mornings. The cottage boasted an immense, intricate television antenna but no television set. The beds were predictably lumpy, the blankets flimsy. There were no decent reading lamps. Agamemnon, normally allotted a cushion on the kitchen floor, was happy with the living room couch. Such is the fate of the rented summer house. On the bulletin board in the kitchen, a formidable list of instructions and caveats loomed. They scrupulously observed them all.

Renting a sailboat that late in the season was difficult; Douglas finally borrowed a trailer hitch from the real estate agent and hauled a catamaran from a boatyard at the far end of the island. "As long as I don't have to get in it," Sue said on inspection. "Double ditto," Cindy added. Tennis was available just across the way, provided they rolled the court themselves. The horses Cindy and Sue longed for seemed not to exist.

They were immediately segregated by their proclivities. Douglas and Bertrand played tennis in the morning; mother and daughter, mutually awkward at it, eschewed the game. Douglas played fiercely and competitively, serving overhand smashes that went wide of the mark, while Bertrand lazed at the baseline, acknowledging what he did not wish to return. Agamemnon lolled in the shade, occasionally stirring to chase a seagull.

At noon when the sun was strongest and the wind steady, the menfolk sailed bravely out of the harbor. Cindy and Sue swam, taking a martyred pleasure from the icy water. For the first few days the dog kept paddling out from ever-more-distant sandspits, always hoping that at this new launch the salt water would have mysteriously turned to fresh.

Sue and Cindy cycled. They pedaled for miles purposefully single file, dressed like twins in blue jeans and heavy white sweaters, each with her hair hidden under a bandanna tied gypsy style. They saved their breath for the hills, all attention riveted on the invented destination, for where, after all, was there to go?

Sue, always a little behind, driving her legs like pistons, made up the dialogues she did not dare to initiate: Do you still love him, your superior Swissman? Are the Alps as perfect as that? Have you left us forever? And received her wishful answers: We are thinking of a divorce. We are thinking of making a baby. Bertie has a mistress, Bertie has joined the Communist Party. We are thinking of coming back to the States forever.

Once, the little general store in Quinig was open; they bought ice-cream cones and sat in a dusty booth eating them. Another time they passed a roadside farm stand, presided over by a gaunt elderly woman who assured them she would have fresh corn—the last of the crop—the next day. The next day she said the raccoons had gotten into it.

"Twelve miles for some mythical corn," Cindy lamented.

"Never mind," Sue said, determined Puritan. "It's *good* for us."

By default they picked rose hips and beach plums and wild grapes and made an overabundance of jelly, filling all the cottage glasses and mayonnaise jars.

"It's sick," Cindy said, squeezing the cheesecloth bag with her purple hands. "Positively neurotic and sick."

"I know," Sue said miserably. "I can't help it." And they picked ticks off the dog after each expedition.

At night they worked by turns on an enormous irritating jigsaw puzzle which gradually pre-empted eating space at the dining room table. From time to time Douglas read them facts from an ancient edition of the *Encyclopedia Britannica.* Everyone wrote letters. "Oh, God, you know what? I started to send a postcard to Goggy," Cindy confessed.

The phone, of course, never rang. Of course, no one came to call. There were three outside edge pieces missing in the puzzle. One night they drove into town and had dinner at the Captain's Table overlooking the ferry slip. Since neither of the men was wearing a jacket and tie, they were seated far from the view. Bertrand, sulking, ordered a twenty-dollar bottle of wine.

"I think it's horse meat," Douglas said of the steak.

"The next one who complains gets to wash the dishes," Sue said, trying.

The problem was, they had a checklist of forbidden topics and they had run out of comfortable small talk. Some of the things they could not talk about included: early marriages, particularly those that take place between foreign exchange students and the daughter of the host family; Cuba, China, or the overthrow of the Allende government in Chile; baptisms, bar mitzvahs, last rites, or circumcisions; America's diminishing oil resources, America's Indians, the American military establishment, Arab-Israeli attitudes, or the Palestinian guerrilla movement; Swiss neutrality in all wars; Swiss bank accounts; Swiss reluctance to grant women the vote. Even Watergate, which they all agreed on, had a way of edging them nastily over the abyss.

This left: pornography, pantsuits, athletics, animals.

Agamemnon had taken to howling at night. They took turns getting up to beat him with a newspaper.

"There's a bitch in heat somewhere on this island," Cindy declared. "His glands get the message even if his legs are too old."

"It's the last thing that dies," Douglas said, leering a little for effect.

"Tomorrow let's take him to the clams," Bertrand said. "It's not too hot at the beach now, is it? I'll bring the termos of drinking water."

"Thermos," Cindy said. "Clamming. You say, Let's take him clamming."

"Please," Sue began. She was going to say, Please don't correct his English every minute, but tomorrow was their last full day together. Until when? Forever? "Please do, Bertie, that's a good idea. If he gets some real exercise, maybe it will take his mind off the call of the wild."

The soft-shells were plentiful and illegal. They lugged away two guilty bucketfuls and gathered up their tools. Cindy and Bertrand took turns calling, *Aggie! Come on, Aggie, that's a good dog!* Douglas walked half a mile down the sandspit, but there was nothing. No blob of blond fur on the horizon.

"He knows his way back to the house," Sue said matter-of-factly. "You'll see, when he's tired enough, he'll show up."

27

Although they managed to finish all the steamers laced with butter and Douglas drank the clam broth, proclaiming it the best part, the absence of Dog pervaded their farewell feast.

Over the dishes Sue said to Cindy, "I don't know what to do. I don't see how I can just leave tomorrow not knowing what's happened to him."

"Oh, God, I know. I feel terrible. But if we don't take the ten o'clock ferry, we won't make our afternoon plane. And Bertie would have a fit; he starts at the university the day after. You know how the Swiss are. Punctual as their watches."

The whole year loomed ahead like a perpetual twilight. "Well, we'll have to wait and see," Sue concluded. "Face the east and pray, or something."

Nobody slept. She heard first Douglas, then Cindy, slip out of the house; she heard the flap-flap of Cindy's thongs on the macadam strip that divided their cottage from the beach-side; she heard their separate, unaccompanied returns, and the murmur of voices from Cindy and Bertie's room. With the first light she rose, dressed, and half trotted the mile to the clam beds. The wind had sharpened; a high gray cloud bank was billowing in from the open sea. No one.

They had coffee and toast and packed the car. Bertrand hiked over to the open fields where she and Cindy had gone for beach plums. He came back shaking his head.

Cindy went along the strip of cottages that formed their little settlement. Most of them were boarded up for the winter, but she knocked at the inhabited ones and left their name and city phone number, in case. At nine o'clock, Douglas dialed the island SPCA and gave them a description.

In their bedroom, facing each other over the stripped and sagging mattresses, Douglas said, "Be reasonable. You can't just stay on here for days and days, waiting for a missing dog to show up."

"But suppose he comes back? Suppose he comes back tonight and the house is closed up and there's no one here?"

"Don't you want to see your daughter off? It's for a whole year. Sue, he was a very old dog. Get your priorities straight. He had a long and happy life. He never suffered. He probably just went off somewhere in the marshes to die."

She noticed that he spoke in the past tense and hated him for it. Hypocrite. Liar. So much for allegiances!

At the ferry slip, Cindy and Bertrand stationed themselves like a pair of Ancient Mariners and stopped each boarding passenger. "Pardon me, but have you seen a big golden retriever anywhere?" Douglas took a last turn through the village, cruising down the side streets, peering into backyards, while Sue called halfheartedly, "Aggie, Aggie! Come on, that's a good dog!"

It was too cold to stand out on deck, so they huddled together as apathetic as refugees in the deserted salon where water sloshed underfoot. No one spoke. Bertrand, who had never had a dog of his own and had walked Agamemnon every morning of the year he had lived with them as a student, put his head in his hands and began quietly to weep.

Sue put her arm around him. He hugged her and cried against her neck.

"Don't, son," Douglas said in a strange and furry voice.

"It's all right, Daddy," Cindy told him, lifting her face. Tears shone on it. "Remember, in Shakespeare? 'For God's sake let us sit upon the ground/ And tell sad stories of the death of kings.' It's all right to cry."

And thus together the family mourned Agamemnon.

The Banquet

Dena Levis—Dena Dillon Gormley Carteret Levis—and I met early one morning on a stretch of public beach in Santa Monica, where I came fairly regularly to walk away my recurring headaches, and she to run her elderly Dalmatian. I had admired the dog, handsomely marked but somewhat grizzled around the muzzle, on several occasions as he loped past a little stiffly, intent on pursuing the tidal smells of smashed crabs and seaweed wrack. This day he stumbled and dropped in my path and lay still in the shallows as if dead.

Although unacquainted, we squatted on either side of him like two squaws by their fallen warrior. I felt under his chin for a pulse and she, seizing his front paws, pulled, crying, "Oh, my God, Melville, Melville!" at which he whimpered and thumped his tail.

Between us we carried him up from the beach to the parking lot; he weighed a good sixty pounds. I sat in the back of her car with his smooth hound's head on my lap and held him as still as I could while the woman whose name I did not yet know careened off down the freeway to the veterinary hospital.

She was a terrifying driver, but with quick reflexes, battling other cars like a Manhattan cabbie locked in a grudge match with a rival driver who has pulled alongside. To distract myself I examined the back of her head, concluding that the blond hair was both dyed and permanented. And I envied it. Dena Levis had style.

Melville had suffered a heart convulsion but did not die of it. Tests showed that his blood sugar was out of whack, and he was overweight as well. On a regime of small, high-protein, low-carbohydrate meals three times a day, he was soon back to romping along the flats at low tide.

Dena's present husband—her fourth marriage had taken place only the preceding summer—taught Taxes and Corporations at UCLA. I was luxuriating in the Dischkoff Chair in the Humanities, where, or from which, I lectured on nineteenth-century Russian literature. All my academic life this had been my chosen field. But the gloom of pre-revolutionary St. Petersburg, the oppressive atmosphere in which fear underlay all intellectual activity, the miseries of worker and muzhik alike, and the pervasive threat of Siberia now seemed elusive and inappropriate in this benevolent climate of mimosas and almond trees.

I had lost touch with the literateurs I represented, as it were. The Russian language itself, that disorderly jungle of irregular verbs blooming among rows of rigid conjugations and declensions, had lost its fascination for me as well. The poetry I had once memorized for its lyricism now cloyed. Pushkin rhymed too facilely. Lermontov was romantic and glib.

Weeks before I met Dena I had begun to suffer from headaches, which I variously attributed to guilt at having left New England in midwinter, and sorrow over the rupture of my marriage a year earlier. I missed the masochism of frostbite and digging out after blizzards, the undignified but comforting bulk of thermal underwear, the whole ambiance of a life tied closely to the changing weather. In the second instance, I missed my ex-husband. The novelty of living alone, at first exhilarating, had worn thin. There was no one to complain to, at least on a regular basis.

We had parted without visible rancor, a bloodless separation after intermittent acrimonies. The grown children, one in Chicago, one in London, applauded our decision as mature, intelligent, et cetera. Even this latter-day wisdom did not rankle. Evan and I congratulated each other on our forgiving attitudes, all of which cloaked, it now seemed, the furies that lead to migraines.

Dena and I were both in our late forties. She had had four sons in two marriages, I two daughters in one. Our lives touched in enough ways to permit us to become unguarded friends. That it was to be a friendship limited by geography simplified matters further. Because we were not bound by long association we exchanged easy confidences. We were able to talk in the purest way, going from conversation to silence and back without connectives. This honesty between us at first disconcerted me, for I was used to the small deceptions that soothe and words that fill the awkward places.

In my borrowed beach house the text I was editing frequently acted as a soporific. So much of the contemporary Soviet critique of Dostoevski was cant, or bowdlerized by censorship. Dena distracted me. She potted, she tumbled rocks, she sang a cappella. Wednesdays she drove up to the UCLA campus for a noontime yoga class. On grounds that it would help my headaches, I was persuaded to roll up my newly purchased mat like a sausage, and we set out together.

Yoga was not entirely new to me. In Vermont, just as Evan and I were so amicably dividing the accumulated possessions of our joint twenty-five-year tenure, I had gone to a few elementary sessions and found them comforting. But here we contorted our spines, we attacked our inner thighs, we practiced rapid breathing to the point of hyperventilation. Toward the end of the class when the instructor began to recite the relaxations, I was ready: "I relax my toes, my toes are relaxed; I relax my ankles, my ankles are now relaxed; I relax my calves, my calves are now relaxed; I relax my thighs, my thighs are now relaxed," up through my internal organs—my liver, kidneys, spleen, and pancreas were the ones singled out for mention—up, ever up torso, wrists, and arms, to my scalp. After that I was lulled almost unconscious when quite suddenly the petite rosy woman who served as our yogi shouted OHM! I outjumped a startled frog. The sound resembled the fervent *ah-mens* of my childhood in church, where they were exaggeratedly enunciated *oh-main*, and I underwent a peculiar displacement. What was I doing lying flat on my back in the chapel?

This feeling of displacement was to become a symptom I perfected during the semester of my burgeoning friendship with Dena. As I came to accept the OHMM, our instructor followed it with OHMM-SHANTI, chanted like a plainsong, and ended by singing, "May your day be a day of peace." Ah, the threefold benediction, I thought, and rerolled my exercise mat.

In our newly acquired states of beneficence, Dena and I went off to our semisolid lunch of grapefruit and yogurt and consoled ourselves afterwards with low-calorie ice-cream cones. We fell into a Wednesday pattern augmented from time to time by supper on my beach-house deck or at a roadside steak place where you were assigned a number, and when it was announced on the public-address system, rose to fetch your laden plate. It was efficient and vulgar. The beef was excellent. I began to feel like a true Californian. The steel bands around my temples, which I always visualized as the flexible metal straps publishing houses employ to hold their mailing cartons of books together, eased considerably on Wednesdays.

Little by little and always at mealtimes, Dena gave me the gift of her life story. Twice she had married the same man. She married him for the first time when she was eighteen and pregnant and abortions were neither hygienic nor easy to come by in Savannah, Georgia. Penniless, they divorced soon after the birth of the baby, a boy, and she married a much older man, a friend of the family, a prominent criminal lawyer from whom she fled half-naked in a thunderstorm on her wedding night and sought protection with the ex-husband. I never got up the courage to ask what unspeakable practices she was fleeing. Dena's unflinching recitations convinced me that my life experiences had been pallid, indeed simplistic, by comparison. The fact was, Dena declared, I had not earned my headaches. They abated obediently in her presence.

The ex-husband hid Dena in Mexico for six months. The angry legal spouse suffered a stroke, which Dena defined as apoplexy—"He took an apoplectic fit," she said— and was partially paralyzed. Apparently the paralysis had struck in the right places, for she returned to live decorously in his house until he died three years later. An heiress at last, she remarried her true love, and three children, all sons, followed in rapid succession.

The firstborn son, however, had been handed over to her husband's parents when he was only six weeks old. They kept the little boy from her, raising him as their own. It was her everlasting sorrow, she declaimed, that they had not yet been reunited.

Alas, this third marriage (second time around to the good man) didn't take, Dena said regretfully, as if she were speaking of a vaccination. Thus she came to marry the present law professor. She admitted that she was invariably attracted to members of the bar. She thought they must appeal to some deeply larcenous impulse of her personality, just as hypochondriacal women are driven to seek doctors as their husbands.

The one fixed star in her life, and the last story Dena told me, was her cousin, her first cousin Howland Blair. She and Howie meet once a month in a downtown hotel in the city of San Francisco, where both their mothers now live, stylish widows on sizable annuities. She and Howie enjoy a room-service lunch and an afternoon's rollicking dalliance abovestairs. She loves the fact that they look so much alike; they could be brother and sister, Dena and Howie; they could be twins. Of course Howland is a good bit younger, but they could pass for twins, she swears it. Always afterwards they meet their mothers, who are sisters, in the peach-colored lounge for cocktails. The old ladies order daiquiris or brandy alexanders, and she and Howie have double extra-dry vodka martinis straight up with a twist, which the mothers consider an act of wickedness. Their remonstrations put a delicious edge on the wickedness just consummated. Then they all troop off to gossip over dinner at the same reserved table in the gilded living room, a situation both she and Howie find hilarious. It has been taking place, with few interruptions, for more than nine years.

"You ought to see us," she said over and over. "Really, you ought."

Dena became blowsy and voluptuous telling me this. With each of her intimate revelations she had displayed a cool, self-mocking detachment. Describing her reckless flight into the storm, she had said, "Fortunately, I remembered to grab up my runnen shoes," a reference to her sneakers. Talking about some easy liaison that had led ultimately to private detectives and vengeful pursuit, she confessed, "When the flashbulb went off, my affections took a sudden turn for the worse." Dena always had an eye for the absurd detail that humanized the experience. I realized how much I was going to miss her.

On the way back east at the end of the semester I stopped off in San Francisco to visit old friends, traitors from the Northeast Kingdom, transplants to the gentler climate of the Bay. They had been mutual friends of Evan's and mine during our marriage, and now they balanced on the banal tightrope of not choosing up sides. Through them I learned that Evan was now living with a twenty-eight-year-old dancer—actually, a body movement specialist—in Boston. While he plugged away at his socioeconomic study of the French-Canadians of New England, now in its third year, she taught muscle control. I wondered what kind of delicate balance they had achieved in their twin careers. My fantasies, if I had let myself follow them out of the kitchen down the hall, would have been grotesque. Ohmm-shanti shanti shanti!

Since I was to be in the city on Dena's next ritual Monday and since my friends' apartment was within easy striking distance of the Fairmont, I called Dena in Santa Monica and promised to join her family group that night for dinner.

The foursome was eating poached salmon when I arrived. Dena opened the circle of the table and sandwiched me in between her chair and Howie's. He was doughy, with the kind of thickened middle that pokes out over a man's belt buckle no matter how straight he stands, no matter how hard he sucks in his girth while being introduced. There it is, the bulge, as obvious as a hot-water bottle.

The two dowagers in their gauzy pastel chiffons were obviously sisters, sharing the same aquiline profile, the bleached blue eyes. They even had the same pursestrings about the mouth, especially noticeable when they chewed. I had the sense that something more than food was being ingested. Each mouthful, bought and paid in full, puckered in and was possessed.

Clearly Howie was a good deal younger than Dena. His face was fuller, more sensuous, but the uncanny resemblance was there, just as she had reported it, In his case the same somewhat hooded eyelids were sly-looking rather than sleepy. There was the same hairline with the widow's peak slightly off center. The angle of their cheekbones was the same, and they had the same skewed tooth in their lower jaws.

Dena caught my eyes triumphantly. A drink was ordered for me—a nasty, mean martini, Dena's mother called it tenderly—and I gulped it hastily, trying to catch up, for I felt it was rude to be one course behind. Howland and I were wedged so closely together on the circle that our knees touched and could not be retracted.

"So you're Dena's long-lost cousin," I said to him, mouth to mouth, while she was trilling to the bedecked widows.

"Cousins?" He frowned.

"First cousins who rediscovered each other ten years ago in Savannah," I parroted, already knowing I had stumbled into a lie.

"We're a lot closer than that," he said. "Of course she didn't tell you, she doesn't like to admit to me, do you, sweetie?" Here he took her hand and squeezed it, whether fondly or maliciously I couldn't be sure. "How come you still trying to hide me, darlen Dena? Your own true son?"

As a kind of reparation I buttered a roll, but when I bit off a chunk and chewed it, the dough refused to grow malleable in my mouth. Dena could not have invented a wilder scenario to beguile me with. What part of it was true? Half? Three-quarters? Why not all of it?

"Why not?" Dena said. "You think I want to go around admitting to a great grown boy like you?" She beamed first at him, then at me, my mouth stuffed full of sourdough roll, a specialty of the house. I felt, among the white napery and heavy silver, as though I had stumbled on a banquet being conducted by cannibals and having been served, say, the thighbone of my daughter, was sentenced to gnaw on it to the end.

On This Short Day of Frost and Sun

Charles Marek stood in the kitchen making shaggy mane soup from mushrooms that had fruited on his front lawn. It was a rainy October Saturday, and even the oak leaves were beginning to let go in a gusty west wind. Of course most of them would stand through the winter, purpling the afternoon light so that it suggested the interior of a cathedral, but here and there he could see holes had been torn in the woodlot by their dropping.

It rains a great deal in the Cascades, but Marek, a native Oregonian, was content with the dampness, pragmatically speaking. At the university he had held an endowed chair in mycology for ten years. Although he had something of a reputation as a recluse, serious students from all over the Pacific Northwest flocked to his graduate seminars. He was known as a witty lecturer. Marek's wife, however, could not tolerate her arthritis in a climate so congenial to agarics and boletes and went off to Arizona every September to stay with her sister until April.

The recipe Marek was following was Katey Hallowell's, neatly typed on a 3 x 5 file card. He had never made soup from shaggy manes before. He was not much concerned with the edible properties of mushrooms. Their fascination for him lay under the microscope where, stained with Melzer's solution and fixed on a slide with penetrating oil, the marvelous individuality of their spores stood revealed. He detested having to lead a pack of eager amateurs on a Sunday mushroom hunt along the forest floor. He was an inactive member of the local mycological association, and he avoided all cocktail parties where bits of puffballs were served impaled on toothpicks.

When Katey Hallowell came west from Connecticut to give her workshops on Aspects of the Dance in the School of Education, Marek was coerced by Duncan McAllister.

"I'm not just speaking as chairman of the department," McAllister said, lighting his pipe and sending up clouds of Balkan Sobranie. "You're such a goddam hermit, Chuck! The lady is famous in her field. We only got her out here because she's a mushroom freak; she wants to go—what does she call it?—foraging. Man to man, Chuck. Help me out. At least come over to the house tonight and meet her."

They were all sitting on the floor when Marek arrived: School of Ed people, the basketball coach, two instructors in the English Department whom he knew and liked, and a sprinkling of students. He accepted a bourbon and soda and stationed himself near the door. The living room was dark, the fireplace smoked, but there was an air of enchantment so pervasive that he soon was drawn into the group.

Katey Hallowell was tiny. Her face was not young. She wore dangling earrings. Her hair was done in a single black braid that hung forward over one shoulder, and she was barefoot. As she talked he noticed that her toes worked as expressively as her hands.

"I hate being called a dance therapist," she said. "Because the same principles apply to everyone, not just to exceptional children. The approach is a little slower, a little more basic, not as subtle, but the joy is the same."

"That's the ingredient, isn't it?" McAllister asked. "We say skills, you say joy."

She was firm. "To learn how to use your body, to find your own space and push out into it, that's joy."

When they were introduced on two feet, Marek had literally to learn down to talk to her. Unaccountably, he felt less shy than he had expected. "I hope you don't feel dragooned," she said. "Duncan tells me you're terribly busy. But I came on purpose during the rainy season, and there's so much you could teach me."

It amused him to think of this mild October as a rainy season. "Saturday, then? I don't have any classes." He found himself adding, "I'll bring a picnic lunch. We can make a day of it."

"You're an angel," she said. "No, I mean it, you're very kind. I hope you'll come to the workshop tomorrow. It's at two o'clock, in the gym."

He had no intention of going, but he nodded. "I'll try."

At two the next day, as if drawn by some phototropism to an unknown light source, he wandered over to the gym. *Joy,* she had said. It suggested a foreign country. The group was just getting under way. Forty people sat stiffly on the floor, their backs to the wall. Katey Hallowell, barefoot and in a black leotard, squatted in the center. Light glinting from her enormous earrings made her appear even more fragile and childlike than he had remembered.

"Now I want to ask all of you to take off your shoes," she was saying. "And put down your pocketbooks, if you're carrying them. Since most of you are teachers, let me point out to you what is happening. You're all pressed to the security of the wall there. You feel comforted. We're always afraid of putting ourselves into the empty space in the middle."

There was no place to stand without being conspicuous. Marek sat down and took off his shoes. The floor was cold and waxy.

"Come make a circle and hold hands," Katey directed. "You see how uptight we are about using our bodies? The circle is the most natural form for a group to take. In it you can see each other and share with each other."

The hand on his left was young and flaccid. On his right he touched Duncan's tough fingers and was ashamed.

"Divorce yourself from where you've been, from your cars and classrooms. Close your eyes and rub your hands together. Feel the warmth of them? It's energy! Now send that energy around to the hand on your left and the hand on your right. Listen to your own breathing. Let your belly balloon out, pull it in so it empties. Keep your eyes shut, everyone."

He wanted to flee. He wanted the floor to fold under him and let him drop down, out of sight.

They progressed to stretches and warming-up exercises, then to walking out of the circle and in, touching toes barefoot. It was not a solemn occasion.

"You see why you're all giggling," Katey said. "It's the sensuality of touching, you see how we defend ourselves from it. Now we can understand why our kids giggle and squirm."

She had them—oh, further embarrassment—lie down on their stomachs. Now her voice descended to his passive body. "This has to do with coming from the earth as an amoebic form," she told the group. "You must push out into space, pull away from gravity—that's it—and let yourselves be pulled back. Wiggle over and touch your partner, wiggle back to your own space. Arch and relax. Now everybody up! Walk as you feel. Find someone whose walk feels good to you, get into couples, move together. Adapt to each other." And she began to tap out a rhythm on a flat leather drum.

Marek, who had felt suffocated on his stomach, began to loosen up. Passing Duncan, he smiled at him and began a sort of patty-cake gesturing with a plump open-faced girl opposite him.

When he was a child in Klamath he had often been taken by his parents to the Grange square dances. The excited rhythm of the fiddle compulsively repeating itself, the heave and jounce of breasts and paunches as farmers' wives and loggers and tradespeople swung in and out of their figures, had made him seasick. He had always stayed near the door, ducking out from time to time to take deep breaths of the frosty air. And then the war came and the dances were discontinued and he was already hunched over a microscope. No, he had never been a dancer. And now his pelvis gyrated and his arms swayed; someone else had taken up the drum and he moved in thoughtful undulation face to face with Katey. He felt bound to her not by love but by blood. He felt hopeful, adroit; at the same time he was overwhelmed with lassitude and longed to lie down.

She walked back with him afterwards to his lab, she in her leotard and elfin black slippers, he in the tweed jacket of a tenured professor. Here he prepared a few of the commonest slides—a russula, a clitocybe, an armillaria—for she had, she said, never seen a mushroom spore under magnification. He was touched by how much she knew, even though she mispronounced the Latin names.

"It's because I've never heard them said out loud," she explained. "I only know what I've learned from books. Oh, and six field trips the Connecticut Wildflower Association ran one year."

They progressed to dinner in Eugene, stopping first at her motel so that she could change into what she called

city clothes. He waited in the lobby, examining travel bro-
chures that exhorted him to come to Britain, tour Paris, or
ski at Davos. He could not believe his exotic good fortune
and was surprised at the appetite with which he con-
fronted his sirloin steak. It was an old-fashioned kind of
restaurant with big glossy photographs of movie stars who
had supposedly once eaten there and given this testi-
monial of their enjoyment. Nostalgia for Clark Gable and
Lana Turner, Ida Lupino and Cary Grant loosened their
tongues, and they exchanged a good deal of biographical
information.

Katey Hallowell had been married twice, both times to
dear, feckless men. The first one drank and the second one
gambled and she still loved them both a little in a de-
tached way. She missed them on wintry Sunday afternoons
with the *New York Times* unmussed beside her, or some-
what more acutely at the holiday season. Twice a year—at
Christmas and on her birthday—she heard from them, and
she was grateful that neither bore her any ill will. There
had been no children, but her work was child centered and
she had five nieces and nephews besides. She was a gour-
met wild mushroom cook. Her chanterelles baked in cream
were famous all over Connecticut, and she had invented
a way to prepare coprinus soup—any coprinus, but she
favored the shaggy manes—that was marvelous fresh but
would keep for months in the freezer. The only trouble
was, she confided, the gray color. "Gray as an elephant's
hide," she said. "I've tried a dozen things to change the
color, but the trouble is, anything I add adulterates the
taste." He pondered this.

He pondered the circle he had sat in touching his cold
toes to the toes of perfect strangers, and the lustful gyra-
tions that had seized him, urgent as the drum beat. He,
Charles Marek, who had married once in the year of his
majority and had fathered upon his suffering wife a son
who was a physicist in Texas and a daughter who was away

in boarding school. He liked to make furniture in the basement while his wife wintered in Arizona. He had made seven coffee tables and a Spanish settee with carved arms, and he knew the names and characteristics of all the trees indigenous to the Northwest.

He slept restlessly that night, mocked by his dreams, rose at seven, breakfasted, and packed a picnic lunch. Katey was waiting in the lobby when he pulled up to the hotel entry. They drove almost an hour into the sullen foothills to an overlook. The day was blustery, a water-color sky threatening showers, and he had wisely brought along an extra jacket. It enveloped her like a greatcoat, and when she thrust her hands in the pockets he suddenly thought of long lines of refugees, soup kitchens, the solitude of his winters. He rubbed his own hands briskly together before shouldering the pack.

On the way down into the gorge, he led, turning from time to time to make sure she was following. She was agile and quick, and bent once to retrieve a pale violet mushroom with violet gills. She brought it to him wordlessly.

"Know what it is?" he asked her.

She held it to her cheek. "I think it's *Laccaria laccata.* See?" And on tiptoe pressed it to his face. "Feel it on your skin. It always feels colder than any other."

It *was Laccaria laccata,* but he had never heard the folk tale of its lower body temperature. His cheek burned where she had touched it.

Halfway down the steep path he found a scattering of *Cortinarius collinitus* and presented her with one. She received it gravely, observing the rusty orange cap, the ragged remnants of veil, and paid special attention to the stalk. "Bracelet cortinarius?" she asked.

She was right. He couldn't resist giving her a little pat of approval before they went on.

It was warmer along the creek bed. The water was lively, but narrow enough to crisscross as they moved upstream.

Marek thought he would collect some fresh specimens for his lab students while he was about it. He worked methodically, prying fungi loose with a quick twist of the knife, identifying each for her, genus and species, rolling the clusters into small cornucopias of newspaper and settling them in his pack. Katey produced a pad of paper and a pen and took serious notes of their field characteristics as he talked. She was like a bird watcher recording her sightings. He felt beneficent and peaceful, and he wished the day would never end.

They ate their bread and cheese on a fallen log. The sun came out briefly and turned the apples golden. Uncapping the thermos of coffee, he thought unhappily that he should have brought a bottle of wine, but resourceful Katey produced two miniatures of scotch. They laced their plastic cups with the liquor and drank to new finds.

"What do you want to see that you've never seen before?" he asked her.

"Well, the beefsteak mushroom, for one. *Fistulina hepatica.* I've looked and looked but I've never found one."

"Neither have I," he had to confess.

"And *Lactarius deliciosus.* I'd know it in a minute if I ever saw it. I mean, I've seen a thousand pictures of it."

"I can't promise," he said. "But I know where to look."

Half a mile upstream the gorge widened into a bowl. They climbed up the north slope, gentler here where hardwoods were mixed among the conifers. He stopped and waited for her to come alongside.

She put both hands to her face in a gesture of what? Dismay? Joy? When she did not move, he went forward a few steps and brought her back the largest specimen. She slit the gills with her thumbnail and watched the orange latex ooze from the green bruise, tested it with her tongue, and still she did not speak. Finally he realized she was crying.

"Oh, come on," he said, mortified. "Come on now."

And then, feeling awkward as a Boy Scout, he drew her to him and kissed her.

They sat among the lactaria and kissed until the sun disappeared behind the west slope, and then they drove back to the motel in Eugene. They were both chilled from their excursion and made love in an awesome tangle of bedclothes. Afterwards, she spread all his mushroom specimens on the bureau to dry and frowning, referring to her notes, identified each one again. Her hair, unbraided now and somewhat tousled, hung down her bare back to the cleft of her buttocks. He was silent. Every comparison for that dark waterfall that came to his mind was banal. She was his naiad; he was bewitched. Later, when Room Service delivered their hamburgers, he was shy as a schoolboy and went and stood in the bathroom until the waiter had gone.

He tried to tell her something of this, but he was a man unused to dalliance and he could not find the right words.

"I read something once," she said, trying to make it easier, "something I've never forgotten. It was by Walter Pater."

He was disappointed. "You mean burning with a hard gem-like flame?"

"No. The same man, though. It goes like this." She took his hands and folded them inside hers so that the energy passed left to right and recited: " 'Not to discriminate in every moment some passionate attitude in those about us is, on this short day of frost and sun, to sleep before evening.' "

It was then past midnight. Clearly, they were wide awake.

She was a traveler, Marek thought, a stranger in his bed. Actually, it was her bed, her Holiday Inn, but he had slept alone for so long that he woke every hour to assure himself that she was still there, or rather that he was still here.

In the morning they shared her toothbrush and he took

47

her to the airport. What could he say? Thank you for the two most quixotic days of my middle age? Thank you for a strange and wonderful time?

"I'll write," she said. "We'll keep in touch. You're a lovely man, Charles."

He watched her disappearing back, her lithe and tough little self as she went down the runway to the plane.

She wrote, as promised. Each time after a decent interval he answered, hoping always that some consultancy would take him east or her west. A year wound down like a clock's hands. Early the following October she sent him the shaggy mane recipe. "After they've all stewed down to an appropriate mess, be sure to buzz them in the blender for a long time. Otherwise the soup will have a disagreeably grainy texture." Then some lines about her new appointment to the Division of Mental Health. Then the news that sank like a stone in his gut: ". . . a widower with two half-grown children. He is a quiet, kind man with the same capacity for joy in his work—he's a mathematician—that so attracted me to you. We're getting married on Saturday in Middletown. Luncheon afterwards with guess what? Shaggy mane soup. Please, Charles, wish me luck this time round. As I wish you, for always."

When the soup was finished, Marek poured it carefully into pint containers, sealed and labeled them, and set them aside to cool. Later he would put them in the freezer where, as Katey had assured him, they would keep for months.

The Perfect Body

A perfect body can be disappointing. I had one once when I was fourteen and fifteen and I tortured it every afternoon except Sundays in the acid-green waters of the Y pool. There, under the glacial, unwinking eye of the Woman's AAU coach, I toiled back and forth training for the 200-meter butterfly. After I won only two out of seven starts, he switched me to backstroke, where I learned to do flip turns and fling my arms up so far behind my head that it seemed they might leap out of the sockets of my perfect body. The following year he turned me over like an emancipated turtle and allowed me to train for the 400-meter freestyle.

Thus it was acknowledged that I was a long-distance swimmer. The swimmer who goes the distance is continually testing will against muscle; I had both and was praised for them as one might praise a towheaded child for its blondness or a racehorse for its long legs. A slow starter, they said of me, but with heart.

My perfect body grueled up and down the lane doing laps with the kickboard. Then I dragged my dead legs tucked in an inner tube while I stroked another twenty laps. Evenings, my fingers wrinkled like raisins, my blood-shot eyes saw haloes around the desk lamp as I sat in that circle of light and conjugated Latin verbs.

My father frowned. He disapproved because my hair was always wet at dinner. Water was an unnatural element for a nice wholesome girl from a good family. He had a more contemplative life in mind for me: botany, fashion design.

"Pa, it's economy of motion. It's grace," I defended.

"You're dripping onto the roast beef," he pointed out. "You'll get water on the brain. Who needs a perfect body? The body dies, the soul lives on."

After the illusion of Olympic fame had faded, I swam anyway, to make my breasts bigger and to work on problems. Every morning the summer I was sixteen I swam half a mile out to the point where the lake bent its elbow and half a mile back, between reveille and breakfast. Once I had settled my mechanical self into the rhythm of the overarm crawl, I could let my mind range anywhere, reviewing attitudes, conversations, family conflicts involving my father. But the major problem I worked on was my sex life.

Afterwards, I toweled dry in the boathouse, meanwhile observing my tough darling self reflected in the strip of cheap mirror. My long torso shone palely against the tanned parts. I examined my swimmer's broad shoulders, my swimmer's narrow hips, and, always with prevailing sorrow, my small breasts that neither the racing butterfly nor the Eleanor Holm backstroke nor the Australian overhand crawl had in any way augmented. I pulled on my shorts and the camp sweatshirt with W on the front and, my long hair dripping onto its absorbent cotton surface, sprinted uphill to the mess hall just before the sliding doors were latched.

By this time Jimmy, languorous, blond, composed, would be serving the oatmeal to his table of ten-year-old boys. We would exchange a secret glance as I slipped past and took up my own caretaking post among the nine-year-old girls. Although we were only unpaid junior counselors, we did the work of the senior staff, who were thereby privileged to sleep through the first meal of the day. God knows how they had spent their evening leisure hours.

Jimmy and I spent ours on the boathouse floor doing roadwork on each other's bodies on a green blanket and hiding under the canoes when the watchman came round each hour. The single beam of his flashlight bobbed once around the walls, slid as though greased over the upside-down canoes gently creaking on their racks, and then tunneled back into the night. Dusty, terrified, but exalted by the danger, we returned to our ardors, two virgin geographers mapping a new landscape. We traveled up the Nile, as it were, as far as we dared, and returned groaning from the expedition.

From Jimmy in the daytime I learned how to tip, breathe under, and right a swamped canoe; how to do the jay stroke, back water, and, standing on the gunwales, rock the canoe forward in a feat that was called kangarooing. I was fierce about these water skills conducted alternately in the black Lastex bathing suit with open-stitch side seams, the brown Lastex bathing suit, its twin, and the blue cotton tank suit, relic of my racing days. These were my daytime wardrobe. Evenings, in the boathouse, I favored sloppy joe sweaters and the camp regulation wool slacks, which itched but were impervious to mosquitoes. From my long hair, drip-drying reluctantly all night, little rivulets ran down the sweater, but if he noticed this detail, Jimmy never mentioned it. We moaned and caressed and involved ourselves in long wet kisses, but I cannot remember that we ever had a conversation. Our heads seemed not to be connected to the contorted grappling in which our bodies engaged with so much pleasure and anguish.

The moral suasion that kept us from going all the way was simple: My father would kill me if I got pregnant. Not with his anger, but more likely with a gun. And Jimmy's father would kill *him*, not with a gun but with reproaches and rending his garments.

Fathers were not taken lightly. Contraceptives were hard to come by if you were sixteen in the Adirondacks. August ended; we parted, unconsummated lovers. After a brief flurry of letters between New York and Boston, the madness subsided. We did not see each other again.

I thought of Jimmy fleetingly many times down the years, and often in warm, celebratory ways. I heard that he had married, as had I—good! Two trips up the Nile to its source. I heard that he had divorced, remarried, gone into film making, that he had received a prestigious award but little money. Then I read in *Time* magazine that he had struck it rich with a commercial film about athletes in training for the Olympics.

The picture was called *Going the Distance*; it seemed to follow me everywhere that fall. I traveled a good deal, taking planes to and from meetings at opposite ends of the country, where college administrators chewed distastefully on the gristle of affirmative action. In every university community I visited it seemed that *Going the Distance* gleamed from the marquee. It had been nominated for ten Academy Awards. It was electrifying, dynamic, revealing.

Finally, in Austin, Texas, I slipped into the 5 P.M. showing. The film's credits marched up the screen superimposed on a moving collage of old-timey snapshots that could have been taken with a Brownie camera. There were wiggly bobsledders, evasive runners, equestrians and skiers half off the frame, speed skaters bent almost double over the ice, a pole vaulter blurring, writhing over the wire, his mouth open in a Münch-like scream, five or six imperfectly stopped shots of a diver executing a two-and-a-half somersault, piked. And then a girl straddled the thwarts of a canoe, holding a paddle for balance. She was wearing my old black Lastex bathing suit, the one with the fagoted seams, and she squinted into the sun. Later, there arose another shot of her shinnying out of the water onto the dock, like an intelligent fish. She was wearing my hair, my swim barrette. I thought I glimpsed her once more, grinning, coiling the rope of a life preserver, but just then the credits paled, the true technicolor, music-laden film began.

Goose bumps began on the back of my neck and spread down my arms. Astonishingly, I crumpled weeping in the darkened theater. What was I grieving for? My repressed adolescence? The lost, perfect body I had not thought of in years?

Flying east, I had to share my block of three-abreast seats with an enormously obese man. I huddled against the window. He sat wedged in the aisle seat, but parts of him spilled over in all directions. *Tiny*, his companions called him, bustling around him, serving him like worker ants. They were fertilizer salesmen returning from a convention in Austin; Tiny directed their division.

Tiny's waist was so capacious that the stewardess had to add a girth extender to his seat belt. He could not fold down the tray table in front of him, but ate cheerfully while balancing the tray with one hand. His bulk, his mounds and hummocks and creases, both fascinated and repelled me. I was particularly struck by the rapidity of his breathing. He labored like the pistons of an old steam locomotive chugging uphill. Even his eyelids were pudgy, and I could smell his sweat. It was sour, greasy, not the sweet sweat of a workout.

An hour before we were due to land in New York, Tiny

became dizzy and markedly short of breath. His friends clustered around, fanning him. The stewardess and co-pilot brought emergency oxygen. There was no place to lower this mammoth creature to a prone position even if two people could have lifted him, but they held the mask and he inhaled, bracing himself as if these were ammonia fumes.

Fortunately, he rallied, then felt well enough to joke with his buddies about his "fix." It was not, apparently, the first time.

I couldn't stand it any longer. "God gave you a perfect body," I raged at him, "and look what you've done with it!"

"It's glandular," he said. "I been this way all my life."

"Glandular, like hell! Wire your mouth shut for a month and see how glandular it is!"

If it hadn't been for the incident of the fat man, I might not have called Jimmy in New York. Actually, I dialed his home phone as a lark, expecting at most an answering service, for it seemed doubtful that he would still have a listed number.

When his own voice came over the wire, I was taken aback. I stuttered, identifying myself.

"My *God*," he said. "Oh, my *God*," as though I had given him some grave news. His concern touched me. Suddenly I wanted very much to see him again, to see how he had withstood his glands, so to speak.

They were giving a cocktail party that Sunday. Would I come?

It was a magnificent duplex apartment just off Central Park West. Everything in it was larger than human scale, from the mural-size acrylic paintings to the furniture, several weighty and important couches squared off in conversation groups around slate tables. The highball glasses were heavy enough to use for cracking nuts; the vodka was poured carelessly, inches deep, into them. The guests seemed elaborately costumed and the women appeared to be wearing stage makeup. They were cinema and theater and dance people and they moved flamboyantly, with large gestures that matched the setting, unlike the deans and department chairmen of my daily experience.

It took me some minutes of hunting to find Jimmy. I was increasingly uncertain that I would know him if we collided. But when he moved back into the main room from the alcove, he was much as I remembered him, still loose-jointed and reedy in that boyish way, only bonier now. His eyes sat back more deeply in his head and his soft blond hair had all evanesced, leaving only a fringe around the crown, like a pale monk's tonsure. We embraced and I realized with terrible sorrow that we were old, both of us: old, with old children. All our fondling and nibbling in the boathouse of Camp Wahmayah had taken place in a state of innocence that now seemed incomprehensible to me. It occurred to me that my own children—and very likely Jimmy's—would be baffled by the limits we had set night after night, wrestling on the green blanket with its raised monogrammed W. This generation, my daughters among them, coupled with their lovers and parted and came together in new combinations with what I regarded as the agility of amoebas. How healthy they all were, and how heedless! What nostalgia, out of that summer, had taught me to number my days? Once there had been a boundless quality to possibility. Now we had come down to the thin flesh under the rind.

I met Jimmy's wife, who was dressed in a gold caftan and wore thumb- and index-finger rings which she clacked together like castanets as we talked. She was square and blocky, like a good child's pony, and easy to be with. It turned out we had friends in common on the Vineyard, we had both toured the King Tut exhibit at the National

Gallery, she had read an article of mine on class-action suits in the *Bulletin*. I felt safe standing next to her and started in on a second vodka.

Jimmy, who had replenished my drink along with one of his own, polished off his martini and went back for a refill. He was enunciating with the elaborate care of the practiced drinker, something I was familiar with from years of MLA meetings with a cash bar in the anteroom. I didn't particularly want to leave the security of the corner where the three of us had been standing, but I let him bear me off on a round of introductions.

"This beautiful woman," he said, and I knew I was in for it. "I want you to meet my secret sex fantasy, that's what she's been to me for twenty-five years, isn't that phenom . . . phenom . . . ?" The final syllables would not be said.

"Believe it," someone offered, and I was grateful to him, hoping it was now over.

"My fantasy object, we were kids together. She wore these bathing suits." Jimmy weaved a little from the effort of shaking his head from side to side. "Kinky," he said. "Under the diving float. In the war canoe! A couple of acrobats!"

It did not seem an appropriate time to ask about the collage of snapshots that underlay the credits. I felt humiliated, but only mildly. I felt degraded or at least besmirched. It was, I told myself, amusing. I could break away at any time. Instead, I let him tow me around the entire room making his announcement.

Jimmy was not quite falling-down drunk when I left. He came with me to the front door and clung to it, swinging back and forth as we finished the amenities. I think we both knew we wouldn't meet again. I think we both felt a kind of inanition and disappointment, not so much with each other as with our age and condition.

I did not ask him what the fantasy was. I preferred to

see it as something lodged inside him, in his neck or head, something rattling like a hard, polished black bean inside his thymus gland or dancing on the heavy veined surface of his retina. I liked thinking that his sex fantasy was a genetic flaw, an atavism, something he need not take responsibility for. Perhaps it had happened like a hump on the back, like a hammertoe, like the gentle uncomprehending sheep's eyes of a Mongoloid child. I could believe he had been born with it, he had already transmitted it through his first-born male son, and I swam off then, as if in the black bathing suit, down the quiet side street to the hailable taxis of Central Park West.

Other Nations

Martha Carpenter's mother lived long enough to paste the names of all her chosen heirs on the undersurfaces of things. Names were taped to the bottoms of the silent butler, the gadroon-edged serving tray, the Sheffield candlesticks, the Imari fish plates, the pair of crystal lamps. She lived long enough to compose nineteen codicils, each in her spidery Spencerian hand, on pages torn from her Daily Calendar. She folded each of these as small as the enigmatic statements that come inside fortune cookies and tucked them into the bottom of her jewelry box, the one that played "Humoresque" each time the lid was lifted. The vanity of her possessions preserved her into her eighty-eighth year, and her life ebbed as peacefully as the tide sucking back from Wellfleet Harbor, where she had summered for half a century.

Three days after her mother's funeral, Martha Carpenter flies to Tucson to address the situational ethics committee of the Pan-American Philosophers Association.

Although she holds a degree in veterinary medicine, the descriptive term Martha Carpenter prefers is ethologist. She is a small sausage-shaped woman in her late fifties with thick, wavy hair that she pulls back loosely into a chignon. Escaping curls soften the hairline around her temples. These gray ringlets and her delft-blue eyes present the picture of someone maternal, soft, nonthreatening. For a woman given to jeremiads it is a useful way to look.

Although her own three texts on conservation, behavioral adaptation, and the ethics of man-animal relationships sell only modestly, she does not begrudge the current spate of folksy tales by veterinarians. All those constipated Pekingese, those Guernseys with mastitis, are grist for the mill, she thinks; they promote empathy. Her focus is the mass production of animals in agribusiness. She flies from conference to symposium raising the issue the Judeo-Christian tradition dismissed when it separated man from the natural world. She illustrates her thesis with colored slides of imprisoned veal calves and debeaked chickens. En route to Tucson today, she plans to rearrange this illustrative material so that the most graphic ones—horses leaking blood onto the highway from overcrowded trailers on their way to the slaughterhouse, 120 lambs dead of suffocation in a railroad boxcar, and so on—are judiciously positioned to keep the audience's attention. In a world that divides out between the tortured and the torturers, Martha Carpenter knows it is difficult to sustain that sense of outrage necessary for change.

The pilot at this moment is climbing to a cruising altitude of 32,000 feet in the skies over Pennsylvania. Martha Carpenter holds four one-dollar bills negligently in her left hand. She has already put down her little tray for the Bloody Marys that will shortly be proffered. There are no direct flights any more. Going west they interrupt in St. Louis or Chicago, in Denver and/or Phoenix. East, it is likely to be Dallas or Atlanta or Nashville. *Serving you in the cabin,* says the pert, vacant-faced youngster in the uniform of a flight attendant, *are Linda, Sharon, and myself, Jeanine. Our flying time to St. Louis will be . . . Door and window exits. Flotation cushions. Should oxygen become necessary.* At the end, her mother snored gently, fluttering the nose tube taped in place, a frail umbilicus connecting her to the green tank the size of a dressmaker's dummy in the corner of her bedroom. It was a peaceful diminishment. She held her mother's hand and did not know, exactly, when the slight breathing ebbed. What she feels now is not grief but an appropriate melancholy, tinged with self-righteousness.

Flying soothes Martha Carpenter. The anonymity of travel and the suspension of time and space, she thinks, exert a calming influence. Outside her window the cloud deck presents an appealingly solid surface, something she would like to walk out on. Here and there, crenellated castles of cumulus detach themselves from the ice floes. It would not surprise her to see the faces of her dear departed ones swim alongside. But heaven has now been pushed so high by technology that it can only lurk on the fringes, far beyond Saturn and Pluto.

She sees that there is a connection between her childish yearning to define and locate the souls of the dead and the astrophysicists' longing to locate extraterrestrial life. Either way, Carl Sagan says; it is equally interesting if sentient creatures do or do not exist on other planetary bodies in space. But the courage it takes to admit the negative possibility! She defers a decision on this one. "A little lower than the angels" is what is in her head, from the psalm, the same one that gives man dominion over the beasts of the field. Over the fowl of the air, the fish of the sea, and whatsoever passeth through the paths of the sea. When she was a child she saw those paths shaped like sewer pipes winding through the Atlantic Ocean.

A child is a literalist of the imagination. She loved then

to debate the issue of heaven and hell with John Jenks, a black man with a degree in musicology, who worked in her mother's house during the Depression as butler and general factotum. Late at night he played Gounod's Soldiers Chorus from *Faust* on the unforgiving Steinway and sang basso profundo in a mournful voice.

The year she was ten, she and John stood by observing while the family fox terrier whelped in the laundry room. The dog's name was Patsy. Martha Carpenter can see again its dear square muzzle covered with bristle hairs, like a coarse industrial carpet. Patsy came as a Christmas gift, sporting a green satin bow. She was not housebroken or, it developed, spayed. In the spring, in her first heat, a neighbor's white spitz mounted her. The child Martha ran home in terror to say that the two dogs were stuck together; no amount of tugging would loosen them. She was admonished not to touch Patsy or to pull Jeff by his collar. Something awesome and inexplicable had caused the grown-ups to withdraw from her. Obscurely, she was at fault. Years passed, she thinks, an aeon, before she was able to connect the locked dogs with procreation. The puppies slipped out, greasy, blind, and fish-like. John helped each one to row upstream to a teat. The last-born and smallest was not right. He breathed for a few minutes, then grew stiff. Martha and John laid the corpse in a cigar box and buried it in the garden. John made a cedar shingle marker for the grave, and on it she lettered an epitaph, her first poem: Here lies the runt of a litter of seven./Since he's not on man's earth he must be in dog heaven.

Much heady talk of heaven—John Jenks had been raised in a Christian Brothers' orphanage, and thought for a time that he heard the call, but proved too visceral for the life of poverty, chastity, obedience. Years later, when they stumbled into each other in O'Hare Airport, Martha knew him at once (she was proud of this fact). Slowly he accepted the metamorphosed adoring child as the woman

61

she had become. He was Muslim now, wonderfully griz-
zled and handsome, and called himself Kimamu Riri. His
silvery Afro formed a halo to that leonine head. They sat
in the cocktail lounge, she sipping white wine, he, Perrier
water. The great compost of feeling between them ran
underground like the mycelia of not-yet-fruited mush-
rooms. They parted at adjoining gates, she flying east, he
west. She remembers that she stared at his disappearing
back, drilling into it for a long, long time, and that he
received the message, the psi-trailing, turning at the end of
the corridor to wave his arm. The fist was clenched, she
now thinks, against feeling.

Philippa, her older daughter, clenches that way, Martha
Carpenter thinks. She is finishing the first Bloody Mary,
preparing to begin the second. Each of Philippa's hus-
bands was a perfectly good man, a man worth sticking
with—at least, she, Martha, could have stayed married to
either one of them—but Philippa was of another mind.
And what a wry thought to cherish in middle age, divorced
these ten years. She is not over that divorce, she will never
be over it totally, however she accommodates, is gracious
and friendly to the new young wife, bears Philip no ill will.
(Despite the civility, she bears him tons.) When Philippa
was divorced, he kept his own counsel. On both occasions.
Perhaps he felt some small satisfaction: No man is a match
for his prodigy? We are cut from the same cloth, harbor
the same dissatisfactions? He is a labor arbitrator and trav-
els a good deal—more, even, than the ethologist mother.

For one summer after the first divorce and over a Christ-
mas break after the second one, Philippa stayed with her
mother on the property in St. Johnsbury. A meticulously
organized person, she huddled by the wood stove that sec-
ond time, cracking sunflower seeds and grieving. Con-
demned to repeat history, was that how she saw it? It
snowed daily. She is a college professor, chairperson of the
History Department. She sits on committees for tenure

review and curriculum reform and has a reputation for unswerving integrity. Her house in Connecticut is an authentic saltbox on the south side of the village common. Sunlight pours into the upstairs rooms. The pine floors, the color of buttered toast, shine with wax. A trio of Siamese cats—grandmother, mother, daughter—rule the guest-room beds. Although she relates less well to cats than to canines, it is a place the mother loves to visit. No television. Orderly, peaceful; the luxury of late mornings abed, a tidy backyard garden. Philippa's files all wear typed labels. When they grow dog-eared she replaces them with fresh ones. The cats growl and mew in a mild cacophony.

Serena, the other daughter, lives out of a suitcase on the other side of the world. Sri Lanka, Bangkok, Hong Kong, Pnom Penh are her ports of call. The horseshow ribbons of her childhood are packed in a cardboard box in the attic in Vermont. In her present life, hungry people eat horses if they have access to them. The market displays dogs and cats to eat, too, when these are available. Morphine, penicillin, rice are in short supply. Serena's whole life is taken up with the zeal of good works. She comes home twice a year, usually in June and December. She was not available for her grandmother's funeral this week. Serena the loosely organized, Serena the militant, a large fierce child ministering to every broken-winged creature, snatching the blankets from her bed to enwrap the mange-infested dogs she claimed had followed her home. Serena bareback in the pasture, galloping her pony under low-lying apple limbs; daring Serena of the wide, wet smile.

In *her* mother's bureau she found, this week of emptying out and divesting, two manila envelopes full of heavy hair. Possibly it is her own hair, once auburn, gone a nondescript brown from years away from the light. She held this strangely dead tangle on her lap for some minutes, searching a way to make it useful, then rose and tossed it into the wastebasket. In another culture, in another time, she would have gone forth surreptitiously, far from the eyes of other villagers, to bury the hair where shamans and soothsayers from the enemy camp would not make use of it in casting evil spells. She remembers her mother reminiscing about how mothers took their infants on their laps to trim their finger- and toenails by biting them. Safer than scissors on those diminutive pink shells. A heartbeat away from the grooming performance of the chimpanzee mother. All our unfinished feelings, she thinks, up from the apes. Down, actually, from the arboreal family. Whence, too, the startle reflex we are born with.

Her mother's unfinished knitting, a memorial to family feeling, had gone to the local Goodwill. There was one sleeve and the back of a sweater under way for the historian granddaughter, pale yellow, all wool, and of a degree of difficulty her mother could no longer cope with. There was a foot-long scarf in burgundy she herself had commissioned. One ancient argyle sock sagged on its tripod of needles, half completed. Intended for whom? A divorced grandson-in-law?

Knitting provides, so her mother always said, a kind of soothing perplexity. She supposes it is not unlike the pacification of a crossword puzzle. She has no talent or patience for needlework of any kind. When in the sixth grade she was required to attend twice-weekly sewing classes, she could not master the blanket stitch. Slipping the unfinished cloth under her blouse, she bootlegged it home to her mother, who polished off the task in ten minutes. For years she had to endure this story, much embellished, as her mother recounted to guests the perils of smuggling, the pains she took to imitate her daughter's ragged stitches.

The hardest thing about old age, Martha Carpenter thinks, is the ruptured synapses which sentence the elderly to repeat the same old anecdotes and not to recognize them in the retelling. And the dependency. She sees with dreadful clarity in the heart of her second drink a long, embarrassing future for herself in which she spins a drudgery of unwanted anecdotes to faceless attendants. She sees again the famous photograph of a dead female chimpanzee, the depressed mature son beside her, mourning unto death. "Overdependence is rare in wild animals. Independence is required to survive," says the caption.

She stayed alone in her mother's apartment the night before the funeral. She slept in the bed in which her mother died twenty-four hours earlier, fitting her body to the space that body had inhabited all those years of living alone. They were both quiet sleepers as adults. A vivid pastiche comes back from her childhood, a night of sharing one bed with her mother in her grandmother's apartment in Atlantic City. They slept head to toe while the ocean snored under the window; she remembers the stucco texture of the wall, the buttons sewn to the mattress, a thousand furtive wakings and wrigglings, her mother admonishing her to lie still.

But this mattress seemed to hold an imprint for her to fill, and she felt no disquiet. She put on a peach-colored nightgown with a Saks label, the top one from a pile of lacy lingerie in the bureau, for she had come hurriedly to this city and in the anguished disarray of the about-to-be-bereaved had packed sensible travel clothes, lecture notes, a silk dress for the funeral; nothing for the night. Even in her mother's nightgown, there was no sign of her mother the night long. She had not been dead long enough, perhaps, to be invoked. Her soul was still strangely situated within a geography of flux; it could not yet visit.

In the night, fire broke out across the street. It gutted the boutique next to the delicatessen, a boutique it had been her mother's habit to browse through after her noontime small lunch in the deli, fingering candlesticks and potholders and scented soaps, the same soaps that overflowed the bathroom cabinet. Because it was a business

block on a main artery, several engine companies re-
sponded. The street below her window was blocked with
hook-and-ladders, emergency wagons, police cars. Snatches
of amplified messages rose on the air: "Over this way,
for Chrissake! Higher, Joe!" A quantity of black smoke
belched skyward, rather like the starting up of the locomo-
tives of her childhood. She could see people coming out of
the apartment building across the way. Onlookers filled
the intersection and policemen were assigned to disperse
them. It was altogether a Brueghel scene at two o'clock in
the morning. A charred smell hung in the air and grew
more concentrated after sunrise.

The funeral took place at three the next afternoon in
the somber parlor of J. M. Oliver's. Philip, a loyalist to the
last, and Philippa were present. Two cousins and the eleva-
tor man and doorman from her mother's apartment build-
ing also attended. It was a lackluster affair. There was no
coffin; her mother had asked to be cremated. The service
was brief and impersonal. Her mother had outlived three
ministers; this one had to ask ahead of time how to pro-
nounce the deceased's name. The curse of old age, her
mother said and resaid to the point of pain, is that there's
no one left. But I'm here, Ma, she whispered, and wept
very quietly into a handkerchief she had taken from her
mother's drawer. It smelled of her mother, it smelled of
her grandmother's funeral and her mother's heavy, mu-
cousy sobs. On one side, her ex-husband in his three-piece
arbitrating suit, patted her arm. On the other, Philippa,
who had been her grandmother's favorite, already wearing
her gold watch, tears shining on her cheeks.

The pervasive odor of char entered here, too. It seemed
appropriate that her mother's life, circumscribed for the
last ten years by these four city blocks she dared to traverse
alone, should be memorialized in Oliver's Funeral Home.
Half a century of family jokes pivoted on Oliver's, on the
black-suited attendants who could be seen slipping into

the alley for a smoke, on the grillwork elevator wide enough to convey a dozen coffins at a time, on Old Man Oliver himself, who wore pearl-gray spats and a vest with white satin piping and was said to be overly fond of little girls.

One life is not enough, she knows that. Martha Carpenter wants her corneas to go into the eyes of the living sightless, her kidneys and liver to take root in the abdominal cavities of the needy. Her body she wishes to be burned, the ashes scattered on fields for forage, the Vermont fields on which cattle and horses now graze in amity and thrift. Nothing is wasted, everything rotates, is composted, lies dormant, rebegins.

Somewhere I have read, she scribbles, *that a will written in a person's hand—it is called a holograph will—such a document signed and dated is legal tender in any court in the land.* When she is dead she would like the historian daughter to act as her literary executor, putting the last unpublished papers in order, exercising judgment as to what stays, what is jettisoned. To the distant administrator daughter she wills the burden of her animals, to place in good homes or have humanely destroyed. Put down, in country terms. It is her fondest hope—she does not say this in the chatty will she is now somewhat lightheadedly writing—that the administrator daughter will return to Vermont and take up her place in the continuum.

All becomes clear. Her pen flies over the page in an orgy of remembering, recording, digressing. Nervous in elevators, wary of escalators, terrified of towers and lookout platforms, Martha Carpenter is secure in this sealed container of measured air and drop-down trays onto which at intervals are slid small gelatinous dinners. One arrives just now; she waves it away, frowning, unwilling to interrupt the associative flow.

One life is not enough. I knew this flying on a Piper Navajo, through thunderstorms, from Minneapolis to

Marshall to talk to the Rural American people. The plane, as insubstantial as a dragonfly, was painted blue and yellow. Aboard, besides the pilot (who was also ticket seller and advance man) and me, a sturdy, youngish type with a wonderfully bushy beard. He alternated razoring articles out of a stack of newspapers with drinking diet Pepsis from a six-pack jouncing on the floor. I could barely swallow my saliva as we were hurled from air pocket to air pocket. The sky turned the murky green of an aquarium. I clutched the skinny armrests so tightly that the roots of my fingernails ached afterwards. Strenuous tail winds buffeted us forward, we bounced down to make an intermediate stop at New Ulm, where I debated seriously whether to continue. Even if I did get to Marshall in one piece, would I be able to deliver my lecture? Bushy Beard persuaded me. We were advancing just ahead of a cold front, he explained. Soon it would be smoother. Besides, not to worry, the Piper is navigable, sensitive, bright—he made it sound like an Arabian filly. Off we went, this time with a third passenger who sat up front to triangulate the radio beam, riding the elevator back up into the strange green sky, rising and falling arrhythmically until my head buzzed with conflicting signals and my entire body was drenched with the rank sweat of terror. My bearded friend sat with his arms around me rocking me like a mothering chimpanzee. When we landed we were told that the area around us had been peppered all day with tornadoes. We were safer in the air. Next day, Edwin of the beard and I were the only passengers on the flight back to Minneapolis. He was the son and grandson of preachers. He ran an organic farm commune in Wisconsin. The sky was placid blue, the sun benevolent. We drifted as in a flat-bottomed rowboat on the pond in Vermont. Edwin's farm specialized in soybean crops, six varieties. We had more to say to each other than there was time for. He took out his autoharp and played for me. Over the comfortable drone of the engine we sang old Baptist hymns, labor union songs, even the "Peat Bog Soldiers." I had never seen an autoharp before. By now I was a little in love with Edwin. Frequently as I board another and another commuter flight—somehow I don't expect to meet him on American or TWA—I look for the soft tendrils of his beard, feeling again how it tickled my neck as he rocked me in the sky over Minnesota.

One life is not enough. She wrote again, in slanting script racing across the page. *"An ethics that does not consider our relation to the world of creatures is incomplete." Albert Schweitzer said that. Take the concept of instinct, how people fall back on it, the way they blame things on Mother Nature, a little humorously. If I am afraid to die on an airplane, is that instinct (we are not, after all, aerial creatures) or emotion? If we say that animals follow instinct alone, it is a comfortable way of distancing ourselves from their feelings. A short step to decreeing that they don't feel fear or joy as we do. Therefore they feel no pain in the slaughterhouse, no fear at the smell of blood or the screams of their fellow species. Descartes, who surely believed that one life is not enough, taught that only human beings possess an immortal soul. In Colombia the capybaras are herded into corrals and clubbed to death for the sake of the meat. In 1417 in the Ming dynasty the Emperor of China sent an expedition to Africa to collect a giraffe, which was thought to be a mythical animal that would bring good luck. Court painters made pictures of it and court poets celebrated it. Now, for every one giraffe that reaches a Western zoo, eight others die in East Africa. Thanks to the so-called capture gun. On modern, fully automated farms, pigs are born, live, and die on concrete floors, never permitted access to the earth or to each other. Farm factories deny animals space, companionship, a life before death. There are moral choices at stake in capital-intensive agriculture! We are the stewards of the lives we raise.*

In St. Louis there is forty minutes' ground time. Martha Carpenter stands in the aisle waiting to deplane. She thinks of the mice in their cages; she remembers a love affair she had here twenty years ago. He was a dashing, opinionated foreigner, a Czech with Slavic cheekbones and a delicate rosy mouth. His field was biochemistry. His research at the university led ultimately to the isolation of a tumor virus. Thousands of laboratory mice died in the two years of Juri's broad-spectrum experiments. Hands that only an hour earlier had chopped off the heads of two dozen mature *Mus muridae* fumbled with her buttons in the nearby Ramada Inn. Martha Carpenter was beside herself, deranged, she now thinks, by passion. They saw each other once a month, either in St. Louis or Pittsburgh, booked into a succession of second-rate motels, terrified lest they meet someone either of them knew. Once they were marooned in Pittsburgh. She remembers her panic on waking to a hushed world filled with thirty inches of new snow, reconstructing the careful lie that had made that trip possible: She was in New York, she was meeting a colleague at Columbia. Only the miracle of a blizzard that had blanketed the entire East Coast, stranding Philip in Washington, saved the day. But the relationship with Juri was tainted by her terror. Her ardor dissipated as the winter waned. Gradually they lost touch with each other. Now, as she walks the corridor lined with candy and cigarette machines, she reviews with nostalgia those tawdry red-plastic motel rooms, the paper bath mats, the scarred bureau tops. Nevertheless, she holds fast to her conviction that we have the right to run risks in our own way, wanting to have it all ways even now. Wanting to be cured of such adamancy.

Airborne again, nonstop now for Tucson with *Linda,*

Sharon, and myself, Jeanine, serving you in the cabin. The litany has a soporific effect. Martha Carpenter dozes, waking to the rumble of the drinks cart, buys a vodka and tonic, and resumes writing the garrulous will. *To left-handed Serena* the gold pin with the left-hand catch custom-made for Martha's great-grandmother. *To Philippa* the amber beads, the silver tea service with Martha's name on its underside. *To Serena,* who may never acquire a cupboard to contain them, the odd-sized Canton plates. As if the handing on of possessions conferred a state of grace. *Once,* she writes, *in graduate student housing in Little Rock I saw mounted on the wall along with some Rouault posters what I thought was a piece of petrified wood. It was cylindrical, jagged, a handsome hanging piece, something that my hosts, a blond American physicist and his Nisei sociologist wife, might have been given as a wedding present. When I asked, the wife lifted it from the nail and put it, back side to, in my hands. "Piece of porch of concentration camp where Mom and I were interned, 1942," it said in small and very precise printing.*

The biosphere is finite! Martha Carpenter scrawls. *It is a terribly thin layer. If I dare to look ahead twenty or thirty years I feel an overwhelming alarm as to the fate of the earth. What is there left to leave? I remember that in Helena I met a graduate student in a wheelchair, a dwarf, actually, a frog puppet of head, hands, chest. The rest of him would have fitted under a dinner napkin. I tried to imagine his life in the motorized child-size wheelchair, his after-hours, his toileting with bags and tubes. But it's a lie. The truth is, I tried not to imagine those things.*

On the last day of consciousness, Martha Carpenter's mother had become obsessed with how slowly time moved, asking again and again, What time is it? unable now to focus the stroke-afflicted eye on the bedside clock. She hallucinated a little, sanely based hallucinations, that the sun had stood still in the occluded sky, was no longer

71

moving on its appointed course. Are you warm enough, Ma? Martha asked her several times, seeing a tremor pass over the bony frame—not so much a shiver as a flutter of moth wings—thinking how the body cools at death. In the casket her father's forehead under her lips had been the texture and temperature of candle wax.

She has read that in the Arctic, in Alaska, in the Yukon, all machinery is silenced at 50 below. What she connects this to, first, and wrongly, is Juri. Then a luncheon in Utah, by the shore of the Great Salt Lake, comes back. Martha Carpenter was seated deferentially with a view of the desert. A young woman told her how she raised snakes for pets, preferring them to dogs and cats because they don't domesticate. Nothing you do to or for a snake, she stressed, will change it. Further—and clearly she enjoyed holding forth on the subject—she bred her own mice to feed to her snakes. Otherwise it was too expensive. She found that the kindest way to kill the offspring she planned to use for food was to put them in the freezer, where they gently lost consciousness. She let them come to room temperature before she doled them out to the snakes.

It becomes apparent gradually that the plane is in a holding pattern over Tucson. The wide, lazy circle it describes is pleasant enough, a lulling effect as of a hammock, imparted by the continual banking on the turn. When they are thirty minutes overdue, the pilot comes on the intercom to explain. A little mechanical problem with the landing gear, folks; we are working on it up in the cockpit and expect to have it right in a jiffy. But in the unlikely event that we are forced to land without wheels, the flight attendants will now review with you the precautionary procedures you may be requested to take. This is just a little refresher course, ladies and gentlemen. We are in no danger. In the event that we make a belly landing, the runway will be cushioned with foam. Snub-nosed

Jeanine, the Goldilocks of flight attendants, takes her place at the front of the cabin and recites from memory the list of precautions. Relinquish eyeglasses, high-heeled shoes. Assume a squat, cushioning the head. Review the safety exits. Review the procedure for evacuation. How to use the slides. Two babies are crying; the passengers remain calm. Stunned, Martha Carpenter thinks, by this vault into the unknowable. We will, as a further precaution, circle the airport until we use up our excess fuel. This process will absorb the better part of an hour. *Due to reserves* is the phrase. Free cocktails are being dispensed during the waiting period.

Across the aisle from Martha, a plump-faced man in a dark green leisure suit settles into two scotches. Just ahead, a woman asks for water, takes two pills—aspirin? More likely Valium, Martha thinks. Detached, numbed, she hears herself order another vodka, this time straight up. And why not go down dazed with alcohol? And why not finish this macabre dance, this last will and testament?

Darlings, what else is there to leave? I loved your father, but not enough to keep him. I loved Juri for his foreignness, but not for long. The next year he graduated to injecting toxic hallucinogens into the bloodstreams of cats. My mother, who left four fur coats behind (mink, beaver, Persian lamb, and a dreadful rabbit jacket), surely thought of the animals that died to put those garments on her back as something like apples, something to be harvested. Whereas I know that animals are neither our spiritual brothers nor our slaves. As Henry Beston has said, they are other nations, caught with ourselves in the net of life and time. *We must solve our population and pollution problems! We must save the Przewalski horse, extinct now in the wild! The dolphins, the whales! And every day farm animals are denied their birthright!*

In the end, they land without incident. The landing

gear has been safely locked in place all that time; the cockpit warning light is attributed to a short circuit. Computer error, mechanical failure, unlucky coincidence, inconvenience. Whatever. It no longer matters.

Finally, taxied to the gate, engines shut down for debarkation, Martha Carpenter looks with longing at the plane opposite, at its rows of welcoming windows waiting to fill with passengers. How shy she has become, newly arrived! She balances the briefcase and pocketbook in one hand, tidily folded raincoat and flight bag in the other, nods complicity to her neighbor across the aisle, and strides forward toward the shifting maze of faces waiting on the other side of the barrier. One of these unknowns scanning the single-file array coming down the walkway will make eye contact with her, step toward her, saying, Dr. Carpenter? And as they walk through the terminal together she will catch sight of the turn-around flight emplaning for Philadelphia. The womb suspension of travel has been ruptured; still, she would like to go back. Even if she was unhappy there, it was a familiar unhappiness. Even though a crash landing loomed, ominous possibility, it was a familiar possibility.

She walks out of the airport, dark glasses in place against the Arizona light. The abandoned will is stuffed in the seat-back pocket.

These Gifts

He was the son of the chief of police of Cape Almy, New Jersey, and she was a carpenter's daughter. They had been lovers in high school, first in the prop room backstage, to which Neddy had acquired a skeleton key—inherited it, you might say, from a graduating senior the June before. A capacious but dusty sofa received them on Tuesdays and Thursdays at four during the entire winter semester before *The King and I* went into rehearsal.

Sheila, who had always been lonely and had accepted it as an unremitting condition of her life, like acne or menstrual cramps, could hardly believe this was happening to her. Nightly in her own room in the center-hall one-and-a-half-bath Colonial her father had rescued from termites and foreclosures the year before she was born, she pondered the concept of selection. With a shy, almost detached narcissism she inspected her body and found it here too generous, there too small, everywhere too blotched.

How, then, had she been chosen to lie down with the daring, dangerous, profane Neddy Linehan?

Nightly at table her father said the grace: Bless us, O Lord, and these gifts to our use, through Jesus Christ, amen. The ceiling light glinted on the aluminum of the wheelchair as her mother slipped crabwise through the doorway to supervise the handing round of the plates; she had been crippled for ten years with multiple sclerosis. Sheila was the Good Daughter. (Anita, the Bad Daughter, had married and left home.) Daddy did the marketing, Sheila the washing up. Once a week she vacuumed, twice a week she ran the laundry through the washer and dryer. Thoughtlessly, almost cheerfully, she performed these homely and necessary acts. Memory of when it had ever been different had faded to a pock-marked, graying snapshot stuck in her mirror frame: Mother, Father, Two Daughters at the beach. Surf in the background.

Barred from the backstage sofa at the onset of spring, she and Neddy coupled even more recklessly on the imitation-leather couch in the game room Sheila's father had built in the basement of the Colonial. Finally, a week before graduation, a little bit drunk and not quite fully clothed, they were discovered on the Linehans' living-room davenport by Chief Linehan himself. His outrage was biblical, retributive, huge. Which had, Sheila saw later with the vivid vision of hindsight, been the idea right along.

Neddy had married her. "Are you pregnant?" her own father had asked, bellowing through the thickness of her locked bedroom door. "Sheila, I want a straight answer! Are you pregnant?"

She was not. They knew a little something—probably more than their parents, although she wouldn't have guessed that fact then. Her mother had sewed every stitch of Sheila's wedding gown and salted the seams with pious, half-forgiving tears. After a weekend honeymoon in Atlantic City, Sheila went to work clerking in a natural-foods store and Neddy apprenticed himself to her father for a summer of tie beams and ridgepoles.

They were young and sunburned and very beautiful—people said so over and over. That first summer, they lived with her folks and sat down in the late dusk to the dinners Sheila had cooked after work, without regard to the day's heat. Yogurt- and ginger-flavored chicken, saffron rice, tollhouse cookies became her specialties. Weekends she allowed her mother to teach her how to put up pickles and jams, a lore that her mother had overlooked in the strenuous years of accommodating to illness and to two adolescent daughters.

The young couple made a bedroom for themselves out of the game room. It was cooler down there, and they used the first-floor lavatory off the kitchen. Neddy had a horror of encountering either of her parents in the bathroom. And the truth was, Sheila could not bear to receive her lantern-jawed, golden-haired boy-husband in the bedroom of her girlhood.

Neddy and her father couldn't get along—if they measured the same two-by-four, they came to different conclusions; when one peered into the window of the level, the bubble never came to rest in the same place as for the other. But the two of them got along better than Neddy and his own father, who were caricatures of each other, freckled in the same patterns on their chests and upper arms, skin that mottled red with anger, neck muscles that stood out like braided ropes, jaws that tightened on words. The same mouth, Sheila thought, watching them fight with words, a foreign way of dealing with each other. But the Chief couldn't take off his belt to lick a married son. So now they swore at each other, father at son and son even more vituperatively at father. Once the Chief squared off and came at Neddy, who had clenched his fists.

But neither struck. Neddy got away before that, enlist-
ing in the Marines and almost at once shipping out to
'Nam. And the Chief softened toward his boy, who stood
clipped and shaven on his last furlough, stood straight-
backed and square-jawed and then marched out like some-
one in a film clip.

Sheila could not stand living in Cape Almy without
Neddy, coming home each evening to the undone house-
work, scrubbing like a nun at her penance. She went off to
live with her married sister in western Massachusetts and
worked assembling condensers in an electronics factory.
"You are killing yr mother. lst you marry that bandit, then
you leave her in the lurch," her father wrote from New
Jersey. She smoothed the letter out and put it in the bu-
reau with her bras and panties, hoping it would soften
among the clean lingerie.

When it was spring she moved to the three-to-eleven
shift so as to have some daylight, she called it, for herself,
and started a vegetable garden in the backyard. She paid
room and board at Anita's, and if she baby-sat with the
two-year-old, it was a dollar an hour taken off her bill.
Strictly business, they agreed, and almost liked each other.
Anita was pale and sharp-featured and looked like a child
herself, coming up only to the armpit of her husband,
Carl. Carl drove big rigs and was on the road a lot. The
sisters seldom got in each other's way.

Things could have gone on like that amiably enough.
Everything Sheila put a trowel to seemed to flourish. "You
take after Grampa Ianella," Anita told her. "He was like
that, the old buzzard. The kids used to steal pears off his
tree at night. He hated everybody. But you should have
seen him babying his tomatoes. Holding the little plants
up in his hand, I swear he *sang* to them. You know?"

"I don't hate everybody."

"I didn't mean that part, dummy," Anita said affection-
ately. "But you got the touch."

It was true. Growing things justified her. Her fingers became pliant and spoon-shaped. Her back ached gratifyingly after a morning of cultivation. She lay face down in the sun at noon for an hour and watched the ants among the grass blades. Bees buzzed in the clover. One stung her and she put ammonia on the sting—some vestigial memory, perhaps from Grampa Ianella. Even so, the arm swelled and a raised red patch itched for days after.

Working the second shift did not displease her. The job was tiresome either way. The other women on the late shift were preoccupied, harried, with little ones at home barely looked after by older ones, with husbands who ran the money off at the racetrack, with depressed or incontinent old parents to look after in the upstairs spare room. Their stories—the inescapable responsibilities—terrified her. She kept to herself and was thought standoffish rather than shy. Meanwhile the beets enlarged themselves to rosy satisfaction; the green beans put up tendrils and from the tendrils hung blossoms of palest violet, followed all in a rush by the pods. In time there was a rich glut of tomatoes. Quite by accident she knew what she wanted to do with her life.

Neddy came back from Vietnam and, because of her place of residence, was hospitalized outside Boston rather than in New Jersey. Combat fatigue was what they called it. His buddy had been blown apart by a land mine as they crawled side by side on night patrol. Bits of his body had sprayed over Neddy; bone fragments not Neddy's own had lacerated his back and legs.

Anita said, "Nervous breakdown: shock treatment— that's what he's getting. You can bet on it." Sheila went by bus every Saturday to visit, carrying her own pathos in a little string bag—the best from the garden, a new magazine, two candy bars. Now Neddy chain-smoked and there were great patches of the recent past that he had no memory of. He *was* getting shock, and his hands shook a lot less after six go-rounds.

Sheila dreamed about a cottage on a hillside overlooking water—a river or a pond. She was hazy on the details of the fantasy but she knew the garden well enough, laid it out over and over in her head, the green beans winding up their tepee poles, the Hubbard squash lolling like big blue babies on their vines. She willed Neddy to get well; if only they could sleep together, she knew, she could make him well.

They gave Neddy a three-day pass. Anita took the child—Carl was driving a tandem rig to Atlanta—to stay at a girl friend's, and Sheila and Neddy had the house all to themselves. She did everything she'd ever heard of to help him with making love, tender and ferocious by turns, but nothing availed and he wept. And then tears worked that last afternoon where all her contrived passion had failed and he came in her, trembling, hoarse with relief.

Even so, he was not discharged until November. They stayed on at Anita's, Neddy baby-sitting days while Anita went to secretarial school and Sheila moving back to the day shift. Now he got disability, which he thought of as a regular paycheck. His hands were steady enough for tools again; he built a cradle for Anita and Carl's expected baby and talked about moving on.

In April they bought an aging Volkswagen painted yellow and covered with daisies and peace symbols. They headed toward Maine, to a trailer and a small piece of land, both on loan from a minister who prowled the wards of the vet hospital. He was an all-purpose, any-denominational idealist with a chipped tooth, chummy with god in the lower case. Or simply in case there was one, a man upstairs.

The disability checks were easily transferred. They bought a chain saw. They bought a sledge, two wedges, a long spade, a crowbar for the rocks, ripsaws and hacksaws, a modest assortment of wrenches, two screwdrivers, and some waffle-weave long johns.

May was cold and rainy. The trailer rattled in the rain, and when the winds rose, it shook along its thin length as if it were once again on the road. Neddy stayed in bed when the weather shut them in, and lay for hours without speaking, in a state so passive that it seemed to Sheila even his breathing had slowed. She thought of turtles, how in hibernation their heartbeats decelerated to dull blips that conserved them through the winter. She didn't much mind Neddy's protracted silences—she had lived without him so long that she could pretend he wasn't there at all. As for Cape Almy, New Jersey—did it exist, now that they were gone from it forever? Her sister in Pittsfield, Mass., swollen with the new baby—was she anything more than a line drawing in a copybook?

Eventually the land dried out enough so that they could get on with turning the soil; eventually she got her garden in. Eventually, too, they fenced out the rabbits and wood-chucks. But she dreamed less of how it should have been. All the while Neddy had been in Vietnam and she had sat at the factory bench assembling condenser plates and tubes, her mind had roamed the landscape, creating a square yellow house that overlooked a pond, a lawn that sloped down to its edge, white geese going single file to paddle out on the water, each one twinned by its blue-green reflection.

Going single file to somewhere—that was what she wanted for herself. Once she had papered every room, arranged furniture, cooked entire meals in this dream place of no name or geography. Now, on a hand-cleared patch of land inland in Maine where the black flies swarmed out of the earth wherever the hoe bit in, she renounced the fantasy.

Hornets had daubed a papery gray cone under the over-hang that sheltered the propane gas tank. They flew purposefully to a puddle, to the nest, again to puddle and nest; their legs hung down in flight, as ungainly as ducks' legs.

When she was stung on the back of her hand as she walked to the clothesline, she remembered her grand-father's ammonia palliative. There was no ammonia. Neddy had taken the car down the road half a mile, to their neighbors'. They were summer people. He helped out intermittently around their place, mowing, rebuilding stone walls, and when he came home things were nicer. There was something to talk about.

She went back into the trailer to fetch a long-sleeved shirt; she would walk to the neighbors' to borrow some ammonia. But halfway there an itching suffused her, be-ginning at her wrists, then the crooks of her arms, then savagely, intolerably, spreading to her crotch. She began to understand that something dangerous was happening and broke into a trot, stumbling down the road. Her face felt flushed; her ears were tingling; something that she could not stop was going on. Her chest began to ache.

Neddy was out back, mowing. The machine made such a racket that she had to run right up to him to make him notice her. But he understood at once what she was saying and ran to turn on the hose; he flooded her giant hives with water and then thrust the nozzle into her hands. "Keep doing it, hear? Nobody's home—the Harrises went to Boston. I'll call the hospital." And came outside again while she was still raining the freezing-cold spray all over her body.

"Okay, we're going." Very much in charge, he took the hose from her, turned it off.

"Is your throat closing? Can you still swallow?" he asked, hunching over the wheel but stealing sidelong glances at her brilliantly flushed and swollen face. They were speeding down the Maine Turnpike, the elderly VW straining to touch seventy, Neddy hoping to be overtaken by a state trooper who would then escort them to the Lewiston hospital.

But no one came to arrest or rescue them, and although Sheila could not speak of it, there was a hard, persistent pain at the vee of her throat. She sat with her head pressed back against the upholstery and held her arms away from her sides so that the air rushing in at the rolled-down window could sweep over the viciously tormenting hives that covered her.

Then at the door of the emergency ward, a nurse waiting with a syringe. In minutes the adrenalin spread through her body, making her heart race as if it would burst. "I'm scared, so scared!" she said.

"Don't be afraid. It's over now," Neddy told her, and took her in his arms, where she gave way to tears. The sound of her weeping filled the hospital corridor—great wet sobs that announced her release from torment as the itching subsided. Then came sobs of gratitude to the hospital personnel for saving her life. And finally came sobs that rose up to reveal her anger at a destiny that had defrauded her; that had dealt her a crippled mother; that had married her off to a daring boy the war had reduced to a dreamlike state, roused now from his torpor only by the awesome state of anaphylactic shock visited upon her.

An hour later, back in the trailer, turning four eggs in a frying pan, she told him she was going to leave him. He nodded; he knew it. He offered to drive her to Lewiston, to Boston, wherever she wanted to start out from. "Tonight, if you want, Sheil. I don't blame you. On the other hand, I think we could make it. I like to think we could start over—if you'd give it a chance." Never had he been handsomer, more winning, more conversational.

"Maybe," she said, trying to keep it light. "Maybe in six months—we'll see," knowing it was never. She would go back to Anita's; she could help with the new baby. Maybe it wasn't too late to plant a few things in last year's plot. Maybe she would meet people, go bowling or something, find a different job, cut her hair a new way. For she and Neddy were even at last. He had nearly died and she had nearly died and she no longer had to stay by his side to keep him alive. Her own life struck her now as much less important—staying alive was a risk all by itself—a dicey, mercurial accident.

She slid the eggs onto two plates, undid the twist tie on a loaf of oatmeal bread, fished out the butter and the jam. "Bless these gifts to our use," she said out loud, surprisingly. How good the coffee smelled! How hungry she was!

A Traveler's Hello

Childhood friendships are an embarrassment, Elizabeth Murphy thought, in the midst of Pamela and Merrick Stetson's New Year's Day open house, in Vermont. I am an embarrassment to Pookie, I am the only one left in the world who calls her that, and I am wearing all the wrong clothes.

Elizabeth was in fact dressed in a suede pantsuit she had uneasily bought for the occasion in Bonwits a week ago.

"I would have known you anywhere, Lizzie, you're still so chic," Pookie said after they embraced, and patted the rust-colored suede cloth. "So Wall Street. So New York perfect." The bones, the scent, the smile tilting to the left were identifiably Pookie, transmuted by—what had it been?—twenty years? She was wearing blue jeans and a chamois shirt. Tanned and attractive, Pamela-Pookie at fifty looked tough enough to shoot woodchucks and bury whatever birds the cats mangled.

"Well, *you* look marvelous, I swear; this alternate life-style, whatever you're calling it, agrees with you."

"Early to bed and early to rise, we're calling it. And you never see any of the regular guys." They snickered companionably. It had been Pookie's father's favorite line.

Thus Liz was launched. A grizzled and hearty Merrick, his hand cozily under her elbow, guided her to a buffet crowned with his own wines. "One hundred and thirty-five gallons this season," he said, pouring her a glass of the plum. "Come on, I'll show you around."

"I suppose you raise all your own vegetables too," she said, following him down cellar.

He nodded.

"And can them."

"Mostly we freeze them. Some we keep in the cold room, parsnips and celeriac and beets and so forth."

"Of course." She would not have known celeriac if she had come face to face with it in the market. Parsnips she thought of as pale carrots; why would anyone wittingly grow them?

"Here's our maple syrup, what's left of it. Another six or eight weeks and we'll be tapping again."

"My God, Merrick! Is there anything you don't do?"

"I have a bad knee," he said ruefully. "The whole goddam kneecap floats around on me. I can't ski any more, or play tennis."

"Poor man," she said, a little unpleasantly.

"Liz, Pam specially wanted to see you again. You ought to know. She isn't well."

"You mean that spleen thing? She looks *marvelous*. That tan."

"It isn't a tan, it's jaundice."

"What's wrong?"

"Here, take some of these up, will you?" He frowned, sorting wine bottles by label. "It's in her liver."

"What's in her liver, Merrick?"

But a new group of guests had descended the hand-hewn open-riser steps for a guided tour of the sauna, the winery, and the root crops, and they were separated.

As if by contractual agreement, neither Liz nor Pookie had ever written each other an actual letter. Since grammar school, they had exchanged vacation flurries of postcards crowded with urgent information. Each of these began: *A traveler's hello.* Early on, the cards ranged no farther than the Statue of Liberty or the Boston Public Gardens. One winter there was a view of downtown Indianapolis, followed by the Lincoln Memorial. Then came the covered bridges and scenic vistas of adolescent summers. During their college years—Pookie at Wellesley, Liz at Smith—written communication all but ceased. Occasionally Pookie dispatched an antique valentine and Liz fired back a hand-tinted view of Mt. Greylock. Conventional daughters of their generation, each married the summer after getting her baccalaureate.

Pookie and Merrick crisscrossed Europe before and between children. There was a traveler's hello from the deck of the *Cristoforo Colombo*; from the steps of the Basilica in Rome; from Piccadilly and Notre Dame; from Cannes and Monte Carlo and the red, red sands of Corsica. Later, a photographic safari in Kenya; another to the Great Barrier Reef. Sequentially, as they attained a manageable age, the three little girls accompanied their parents. It was a period studded with postcards, of energetic, archivable messages. *A traveler's hello!* Not even Peter Pan crowed more pridefully.

A traveler's hello from Selma and Montgomery. From Memphis and Washington, Boston and Chicago. Merrick's arrest at the Pentagon arrived on the back of an aerial view of same. *A traveler's hello from Pig Palace in stitches.* Soon thereafter came the decision to move to Vermont. Details about the construction of this house were scanty: *A three-year project, architecturally incorrect, experts all say too many wings.* With every card, a renewed invitation to Liz to pay a visit.

Liz countered with art reproductions from the Metropolitan gift shop and views of Wall Street. She kept a dozen of these in her desk, for fast retorts. This year, she vowed, she would go to Vermont.

And then in November a postcard from Pookie from Hanover, a view of Dartmouth College. *A traveler's hello from the northern branch of the Ivy League. I'm here to have my spleen out. Nothing serious, but what will I vent with now?*

Pookie and Liz had been friends since first grade at the Parker School, in suburban Philadelphia. All through grammar school they were fierce, unabashed best friends, resisting any separation. Pookie had a dollhouse, an exact replica of the house she lived in, with nine handsomely proportioned rooms and a portico of white pillars. Behind Pookie's house lay a rose garden of sorts and a lawn for croquet. Liz's house, three blocks away, leaned against a corner grocery and fronted on trolley tracks. The local fire station loomed behind. Pookie's sidewalk was best for roller skating, Liz's third-floor back porch for spying on the firemen through Pookie's father's binoculars.

The social differences, Liz had found herself thinking as she trudged up the serpentine walk to the huge cedar country house with wings, the social differences weren't even noticed until sixth grade. "Don't envy me," Pookie had warned her once they were in high school, once it was a matter of cars and clothes and leisure-time activities. "I can't bear it if you envy me. None of it is my fault."

But how Pookie had envied the beer and pizza kitchen of Liz's brown house, the noisy comings and goings of uncles no older than Liz's brothers. The all-time sad, singable lyrics on the Stromberg Carlson causing the bedroom floor above to vibrate with the bass notes. How Pookie had admired the trolleys that squealed and shot blue sparks under the windows all night long, their lighted interiors revealing the solitary late traveler who excited her imagination. And how, on the frequent weekends she was allowed to stay over, Pookie had adored the shrieking of the fire alarm, the scramble of men and equipment, the terrifying siren that punctured all workaday sounds or, even better, shattered the diminished murmur of midnight. How she would huddle on the back porch, rubbing her goose bumps, fascinated with the purposeful bustle below.

Purposeful bustle, that was what Pookie had put into her adult life, Liz thought, rounding the last turn and fronting on the house. She had not dared drive her brother's bulky Pontiac any closer; she would never have been able to park it, she was sure. She carried her house present under her arm, a footscraper with double brushes guaranteed to remove snow and mud from the ridges of the most elaborately soled hiking boots. Most of the cars parked along the shoulder of the hill were Saabs or Volvos, here and there a Volkswagen or mini-pickup truck. A sprinkling of bumper stickers proclaimed NO NUKES and SPLIT WOOD, NOT ATOMS. There was one RECYCLE YOUR GRASS, FEED A HORSE and one J'AIME LE BOIS.

Liz had spent the week between Christmas and New Year's in Brattleboro with her youngest brother and his wife. Her brother, who had been in hardware and sheepskin jackets, now owned a chain of shoe stores. Mostly he carried boots with felt liners and hard-wearing leather outdoor shoes. Very little call for high heels, he would say, sprawled in his reclining chair, pulling the tab on his third beer of the evening. He and Charlene were enthusiastic snowmobilers, they belonged to a club. Everyone wore quilted jumpsuits with the club emblem, a wolf, on the breast pocket. Saturday nights, in season, they went out in packs, ten or twelve in a line.

Liz loathed all holidays, Christmas supremely. She could not fake it at Christmas. After the mid-December rush to

sell so as to take losses before the year ended, her clients—
she was an investment analyst—dropped out of sight until
February. The market dozed. The office, at the end of
December, was one big poisonous eggnog party. She went
to a lot of late-afternoon movies. There was no one she
was close to, as she would say, "at the moment." In New
York she lived without houseplants hanging in the win-
dows or mung beans sprouting under the sink. She com-
peted for taxis and ate in restaurants three or four times a
week, frequently with her ex-husband, Rich, who was now
gay. They went Dutch and discussed the children, one in
prep school in New England, the other a sophomore at
Liz's alma mater, Smith. The difference was that Liz had
been a full-scholarship student. She had waited on tables
six hundred meals a year for four years. Summers, she
had assembled weather balloons in a factory. Sally was a
dilettante.

There were the usual problems. Mark was failing
French. He took his guitar to language lab and played his
original folk songs onto the tapes instead of parroting the
lesson. Sally, with Liz's connivance, had recently had an
abortion. Liz did not tell Sally's father the facts in this
case; it would have upset him terribly. He could not, he
said, deal with aggressiveness in women. Abortion is an
aggressive act. He said this frequently.

For the sake of decencies between them, Liz chose not
to argue. Looking back she could see that she had proba-
bly always known Rich was homosexual. She had seen it
the minute he got out of uniform. She had seen it each
time he reached for the second drink, when something
loosened and changed direction. He was tender and non-
bitchy and she loved in him precisely the qualities that
directed the amorous force of his attention away from her.
After ten years of leading a double life, he came out of the
closet. The children were told in the most considerate way

possible why Daddy was leaving. Neither seemed scarred. Rich left her the hi-fi, the paired tickets to the Philharmonic, a paid-up year of paddle tennis in Riverdale, and a heavy sense of herself as a dutiful pal.

When they were first married and living in the same city as Pookie and Merrick, Liz remembered that Rich's big word was "hostile." Going to bed early was a hostile act. Merrick—she had agreed with him here—had a faintly hostile smile. As couples they had attained only lukewarm friendship. Liz and Pookie did not discuss the gradual erosion of their passionate loyalty; tact got in the way of honesty. Liz never liked Merrick very much. He was a dogmatic man, intelligent and witty but suffocatingly insistent on his own point of view. Daughters, she thought, exactly suited him. She thought he could not have borne the rivalry of sons. She remembered the New Year's Eve they had all gotten drunk together, three couples: Barby and Rob now divorced, she and Rich amiably separated. That night the men had all put their jockey shorts in the refrigerator, she forgot why.

It was midafternoon. An expedition was being organized by the Stetsons' middle daughter to hike up to two mysterious domed rock chambers, presumed to be sacred Indian places. "Go, you'll love it," urged Pookie. "People have been arguing about them for years, whether they're just colonial root cellars or pre-Columbian." Six guests assembled in the entryway. The downstairs windows were now all steamy from animal heat, the living room was chock-a-block with people and pots full of avocado trees. All home-sprouted, no doubt, Liz thought. At least she had the right boots for tramping about in the snow. She was grateful to her brother for the gift. The afternoon was brilliant, the temperature a benevolent 28 degrees. They followed a snowmobile trail for half a mile, then turned to cross a partially frozen brook and climbed along a cut where the footing grew difficult.

Conversation was patchy. "An archaeologist from Yale was here last summer. He said these mounds are clearly Celtic," Ginny said. "Tenth century, most likely." Ginny had one more year to go to Yale. After that, it was to be law school, most likely. The Stetsons' oldest daughter was in medical school at Western Reserve. The youngest grimly expressed no preference as yet.

As they stumbled back down the rock face in the gathering dusk, Liz alternately helped and was helped along by a man with a melancholy mustache. "Madness," he said, falling, and when she too fell, "Insane." Then, on the flat, they exchanged biographies. He was no longer married, he worked for a foundation in New York, and he had one son, a high school dropout, and a daughter who swam. "Have you noticed how everybody's children at this party are exceptional?"

"You mean you've noticed too?" she said.

"Sure. Everybody's children are either in law school or med school or posted to lookout stations to spot forest fires in the Rockies. Aren't anybody else's kids dull normal?"

Liz felt better. "Do spoiled brats count?"

"Friend," he said. "Kindred soul. Tell me you don't heat your entire house with wood."

"I don't even grow herbs on the kitchen windowsill."

"Or distill dandelions in the cellar?"

"Listen," she said, "I eat meat. I live in a steam-heated duplex in the Village and, generally speaking, I make it a point to avoid ice and snow."

A hundred yards from the house, Ginny was waiting for them. "Can I talk to you a minute?" she said to Liz.

Dismissed, the mustache hurried on ahead.

"I don't know if Daddy has spoken to you yet. I think since you're Mommy's oldest friend . . ."

"What's wrong with her, Ginny? I know something's wrong. Is it that spleen thing?"

"It's cancer," the girl said emphatically, giving the syllables equal weight, a word she was learning to thrust into conversations. "It's cancer of the liver. The doctors say there's nothing more they can do."

Liz repeated, "Cancer," but without conviction. The smell of woodsmoke drifted to where they were standing. The setting sun had thrown house and hill into knife-edge relief. Cancer was a turkey vulture flapping overhead.

"Right now she's in her denial phase. She feels well, so nothing is happening to her, you know?"

Liz didn't know. Denial phase, that sounded like something Rich would say. Denial is a hostile act. She reached to take Ginny's hand as a gesture of comfort. Suddenly her arms were full of Ginny weeping.

Liz's face flushed hot with guilt. If Pookie was dying of cancer, then she, Liz, need no longer feel the continual, corrosive, piggish gnawings of envy. Envy is a mortal sin. Envy is for third-raters. Years of it had etched and attenuated their friendship. She had envied Pookie's nose, the slope of her shoulders, her marriage, her loyal dogs. She had envied her clothes, her achieving daughters, her smoothly shaven legs, her convictions, her equanimity and money. She envied her origins, her dollhouse, her College Board scores. Assaulted by self-blame, still Liz felt marvelous. If Pookie was dying of cancer, then she, Liz, surely was not.

In a little while she and Ginny went back in the house. The man with the mustache was named David Lovejoy. He was waiting with a ravenous expression; he had not eaten since breakfast. She was mortified to discover how hungry she was, too. They stuffed themselves with spinach pie and noodle pudding, hot biscuits and avocado salad. No animal had died to furnish this buffet.

93

Liz put off thinking about Pookie's condition. Everywhere she looked, Pookie was in animated conversation, throwing her shoulders back, arching her pelvis slightly in the gesture of laughter. Pookie embraced arriving, departing guests. Pookie unwrapped a pair of oven mitts, a basket for French bread, the Hammacher Schlemmer bootscraper. There was Pookie pouring wine, patting the three dogs, all of them black German shepherds. Pookie with Merrick's arm around her, cozy and doomed.

At the end of the party, Liz and Lovejoy exchanged addresses, telephone numbers. Vague promises were made, the kind she desperately wanted to believe in. For years and years she had been falling through space with an untested parachute. She neither crashed nor pulled the cord.

"Don't come back unless you feel up to it," Merrick said, walking down with her to the hulking Pontiac. He stood there, making small, aimless circles in the dark with his electric torch. As if the decision were his. She and Pookie had had a life before he was even thought of. She made no protest.

Pamela Pookie Stetson lives eighteen months after this New Year's Day, first giving up her uterus, then a portion of her large intestine. She remains cheerful and active after the surgeries, walking with the dogs, vigorously weeding the garden, but she progresses out of denial and into acceptance.

Pookie accepts death the way she had accepted civil disobedience. Then she had learned how to sit hunched over, protecting her kidneys; she had learned how to go limp when arrested, while being carried out of federal buildings and hoisted into paddy wagons. She is doing what she has to do the same way she formed a human chain with other mothers on the cobblestones in front of the Navy buses. Only this time, she must do it alone.

Liz goes weekly to see her, flying up to Burlington, where one or another of the daughters meets her plane. She and Pookie have taken up where they left off, twenty-odd years ago, as if in midsentence. When Pookie is resting, Liz entertains Ginny and the others with details of their mother's childhood. She describes all the unexceptional entertainments of their era and then remembers the two ten-year-olds spying on the firemen in the adjacent dormitory through Pookie's father's expensive bird-watching binoculars. Grown men, scratching their genitals, blowing their noses, buttoning, unbuttoning. Two little girls, too wicked to be caught.

In Merrick's study, a lovely haphazard welter of books and periodicals, Liz is magnetized by one wall of framed photographs. Here are the dogs of a lifetime, prick-eared and intelligent on lawns and snowy slopes. Here are the interchangeable little children in snowsuits and shorts. Here is the house going up, and the chimney of massive fieldstones. Here is the family hauling wood together, digging the garden, posing on skis. The central space on the wall is occupied by two glossies of Merrick himself. In one, he is being quick-marched down the Pentagon steps by a grim-faced policeman. In the other, one arm twisted behind his back, he is being led toward the police van. Still, he has turned toward the camera and he is grinning.

"He was knocked unconscious by that guy," Pookie says, breathing behind her. "Knocked cold about ten seconds after I clicked the shutter. That was Chicago."

Liz doesn't answer. She is thinking about the new Jerusalem in which you have your picture taken for posterity while you are being arrested. Along with the flushless toilet and piles of horse manure on the garden, it is the old made new again. The early Christians were masters of civil disobedience. If Merrick had been burned at the stake for his beliefs, she is thinking, Pookie would have been be-

95

side him, light meter in hand, recording the moment for posterity.

Liz and Lovejoy see a good deal of each other during this time. Once, that first winter, they go to Puerto Rico for five days, and the following autumn to Nova Scotia. The postcards are better in Nova Scotia. *A traveler's hello from Digby! Panorama looking southeast.* Pookie is no longer the link between them, for they have forged one of their own, but it is tenuous. Each fears it will not bear the weight of exposed feeling. They are both scrupulous in this regard, never imposing.

The strain of Pookie's dying causes Merrick's kneecap to go out of whack again. This time it rotates clear around to the back of his knee. In great pain, he is unable to put any weight on that leg at all.

Pookie lies half conscious in the balcony bedroom she loves. Half a dozen bird feeders in the trees outside her window glitter and fill with finches. Contrary to public belief, it is not a painful time. The day before she dies, an indigo bunting appears.

Now it is over. It was over a week ago. Liz and Lovejoy are having dinner together before the memorial service. Lovejoy has cooked a substantial dinner. Merrick, on crutches, has come to New York. He is to meet them at the Ethical Culture building, where he and Pookie were married.

Liz slashes viciously at the slice of roast beef on her plate. She is still hungry for meat, after so much time in a vegetarian household waiting for death. Grief and blood go together, she thinks, but cannot lift the fork to her mouth.

Propped against the salt cellar is a postcard she received yesterday. On the front, a reproduction of a fire engine pumper, circa 1880, from the Smithsonian. The brass fittings, some with elaborate curliques, have been lovingly shined. New black rubber hoses, undoubtedly custom made, are coiled across the back. *Very dear Liz,* Pookie has printed, *I saved this for you years ago, but Ginny promises to mail it afterwards. A traveler's hello from our nation's capital! love always, your Pookie.*

To Be of Use

"That was the most terrible winter of my life," Mary tells Andrew. "It rained the whole month of December, the rain line kept sneaking down from Oregon. There'd be these downpours, and a huge chunk of road would collapse. You couldn't go anywhere. I got so claustrophobic. I was twelve years old and I thought about killing myself every night lying there, listening to the rain beating on tin. We had to postpone Christmas till the end of January."

Andrew is Scots. He is driving Mary back to the school on the North Shore of Massachusetts where she teaches beginning French to his oldest son, Duncan, and eleven other fifteen-year-olds. She is resident proctor as well. Andrew teaches there too. As a diversion, he has developed a college-style seminar in European history which is open only to approved seniors. This is a private school of the second rank. Students do not often graduate from it into Princeton or Yale or Harvard.

"The reason Amelia is so moody today," Andrew tells

Mary, who already knows why, "is she didn't sleep two winks last night. She's still worrying about her orals next week. She can't start on her dissertation until she passes her orals."

They both know she will pass.

"Anyway, she kept coming out of her room and pacing the hall, and then the dogs would get up from my bed and go out of my room and start pacing with her. I could hear their toenails clicking up and down."

Andrew is a big man, with cheeks as uncommonly ruddy as if they have been freshly slapped, and his wife, Amelia, is an American automobile heiress. Amelia is an inch taller even than he. She is fine-boned and stoop-shouldered from a lifetime of slouching, before she met Andrew, so as to diminish herself.

The marriage took them both by storm and they were happy, with matching eccentricities. For a long time, Andrew rode horses recklessly, skied the steepest slopes, hurled himself with ropes and pitons up the rocky sides of mountains. Amelia stayed home to paint great geometric canvases in acrylics. They were rhapsodies that celebrated trapeziums and rhomboids and scalene triangles, and they hang everywhere in the restored farmhouse, even in the bathrooms.

Now the house is full of children. Andrew's and Amelia's styles have changed. Because they keep separate hours, they have separate rooms. "With equal visitation rights," Andrew is fond of saying.

In seven years, four sons were born. They are a race of giants, all growing tall and thin as stalks of ripe timothy. The boys are nearsighted in gradations of severity, beginning with Duncan, the oldest and most afflicted. Perhaps the genes have relented as Andrew and Amelia coupled; Ian's glasses are less thick than Duncan's, Quentin's prescription is even milder, and the baby, Douglas, needs his glasses only for archery and baseball.

Once Douglas was firmly established in the first grade, Amelia went back to graduate school. She is getting her degree in Public Health. Hospital economics, a language peppered with graphs and equations, is her particular focus. Her professors are cordial and sympathetic; they dote on Amelia, who is a straight-A student.

At home, this pale woman with soap-colored eyes has a cool, equable way among her sons that just suits them. Those who wish to bake cakes in the afternoon are encouraged to do so. Those who prefer to roar around the property on two unregistered Harley-Davidsons are permitted to do so. Personal matters seldom come up for discussion. Hygiene is referred to vaguely from time to time; religion, never. All information is imparted in a hearty and detached manner.

Since earning a living is a matter of no concern, Andrew has taken to raising Highland cattle and black sheep, only partly out of nostalgia for the misty, harsh terrain of his origins. More out of chic, Mary thinks. The Alfa Romeo sports car he drives—a gift from Amelia, who frequently dispenses new cars for Christmas—is chic too. He drives negligently, steering with one hand and waving a lighted cigarette with the other. He puts the cigarette to his lips when it is time to shift and stabs the air with it for punctuation the rest of the time.

"Life is dumb luck," he tells Mary. "Blind chance."

She agrees. She knows what he is going to say next, and then he says it; "I'm just a sheepherder's son. A shepherd boy." Always with the same intonation.

Here is the rest of it: "But I was tagged by the system. I was a British subject and the Queen rescued me." What he means is that he took the standard competitive exams at age eleven and was singled out for a classical education. He went up the ladder in the approved fashion clear through the University of Edinburgh, thence to London to graduate school.

"And then what luck to meet the robber baron's daughter," he says to Mary, refurbishing the story of how he and Amelia collided in the corridor, both hurrying to a lecture by Bevan. He, because attendance was required; she, because it was something to do. "I knocked her flat and then I picked her up and destiny took us both in her arms."

The tails of Andrew's lambs are not docked in the old-fashioned way Mary remembers. In California each spring, her father took down from its peg in the barn the stained pine board with a semicircle cut from one side. Held on its back too long, a sheep will suffocate. The weight of its thorax is too heavy for it to breathe against, or so she had been told. Over and over it went like this: Two seconds to throw the lamb, two more to adjust the cutting board. The knife, the cautery to control bleeding. Dazed, trembling, bleating nonstop, the little thing was up and racing away in less than ten seconds. Occasionally, though, one failed to rise, stunned by the shock. Occasionally some of the docked stubs became infected and required daily care.

"And now look what's happening all over California," Mary says. She is from Eureka. "The worst drought of the century. They've cut my dad back to forty gallons a day. He can't keep his sheep on forty gallons a day; he's going to have to sell off two thirds of his flock."

Mary has a mother as well, and a married sister, but all Andrew ever hears about is her dad. He understands that she is fixated on her father, he even understands what Freud meant when he made that remark about four people in every bed. Or eight, for all he cares. Mary is good for him. She has animal tact, she can get along with anything on four feet.

Andrew's lambs wear heavy-duty rubber bands on their tails. Deprived of its blood supply, the appendage withers and eventually falls off. Today there are a dozen suckling lambs to catch and band. Amelia is indifferent to this other world of Andrew's, and he does not ever ask her to help. The boys are always elsewhere when he needs them. Usually, Andrew performs this task himself, holding the wriggling lamb between his legs and folding his long frame down almost to the ground so that he can spread the elastic on the four-pronged pliers and snap it around the tail. It is a clumsy one-man operation. But with Mary to imprison the creature, holding it tight in her arms rather like a large two-year-old child in the midst of a tantrum, the job goes easily.

"God, he weighs a ton!" Mary says when Andrew hands her the last and largest of the lambs. He is three weeks older than the others. "Really! Hurry up, he's a monster." Andrew admires the way she presses her back against the barn wall and hangs on. The little bugger thrashes wildly in her arms. She clamps her chin into the fleece of his neck to help steady him.

"Now we both deserve a cup of tea," he says when they are done. They take the smell of the sheep indoors with them, but instead of tea, Andrew mixes martinis.

Even though gin gives her a fearful headache, Mary drinks hers. Andrew has animal magnetism.

On the other hand, she is twenty-eight years old and has no steady lover.

"What would I do with one?" she asks Andrew, who points out this lack.

"Adjust." Is he getting tired of her? At least, he is tired of bullying her, she is too easy to bully.

"I don't want to adjust."

"Don't you want to lead a more interesting life?"

"Not particularly." She can feel the headache beginning. She hates these interrogations. She doesn't need Andrew to tell her she is out of the main stream. She should be living in Cambridge, meeting people, answering ads in *The Real Paper*. Or running one of her own. WF 28, INTELLIGENT, FLUENT IN FR., INTO SHEEP, SEEKS APPROP. M FOR

COMPANIONSHIP OUTDOORS & IN. It isn't that she longs to continue the family tradition. She doesn't expect to raise sheep all her life. It's just something she knows, the way other women know the Goldberg Variations, or how to fire a kiln or tell a real antique from a copy.

Andrew's lambs are castrated with elastics too. The thought of all those miniature testes falling off like abandoned eggs somewhere in the pasture makes Mary's flesh creep. She isn't sure why. Does it seem medieval, crueler, this slow, supposedly more humane procedure, than the bloody ritual full of terror that she remembers? Afterwards, the lambs sprawl on the earth and bite at the elastic, but they do not bleat and bleed and run in crazed circles.

The shepherds of his childhood, Andrew tells her, Andrew delights in telling her, castrated their ram lambs by biting off the scrotal sac and sealing the cut with their own tobacco-chewing saliva as antiseptic. Somehow, although grotesque, this is an act in nature she can accept. More than once she had been assigned to catch a ewe's urine in a jar, then liberally sprinkle a newborn triplet with the rank, yellow dribble so that the poor shut-out lamb would smell like its foster mother and be allowed to suck.

Sheep are dim; everyone agrees on this point. Yet they knew the slaughterer's truck before it turned into her father's lane. They seemed to have a sixth sense for the culling of the flock just as they had for a weather front brewing, and they rushed about blindly, forming their football huddles in corner after corner.

Unlucky enough to be born white in Andrew's domain consigns a lamb to be eaten. The barren ewes are likewise dispatched. But for the stalwart black ram and the complaisant Cheviot ewes upon whom he begets generations of black lambs, there are safety, hay and grain, and warm winter quarters.

Now it is dark. Andrew and Mary fly over back roads to the Rendham School. Somewhere in this last five miles Andrew will pull off the road and press the button that puts up the top of his spiffy, hand-finished car, and there in the cramped dark he will exact from Mary his reward: for what? Release from the boredom of a boarding-school Sunday. Dinner, fragmented and jazzy under the cobwebbed chandelier—the house goes scandalously undusted—where Amelia frowns and appears to be memorizing logarithms as Andrew carves the roast. Embarrassment as the stair-step boys, smelling faintly of sheep dung and last week's underwear despite their putative Sunday baths, giggle and punch one another in the secret ceremonies of all brothers.

Mary does what is expected of her because Andrew makes her homesick. And because she is convinced that she and Andrew are second-raters. He has had the wit to marry above himself. She, by her own bootstraps, has come out of northern California, through the state university system, to support herself. She taught first in a school in Michigan. After two snowbound winters on the Upper Peninsula, she arrived in this place. Which is, after all, an eastern boarding school of some repute. She is the envy of her sister, the cynosure of her entire family. She has been teaching all year at Rendham and going home for Sunday dinners with Andrew since February.

"It's not going to work out," she told him, that first time, but he paid no attention to her.

"I'm not clear what's happening to us," she ventured later, although by then she was buttoning her blouse.

"What are you trying to tell me?" he asked. "Are you sorry?" and there was no answer to that. She thought at first he was too upper-class, too imperious, also too offhand to bear. But when she heard his humble sheepherder's story, when she saw him standing among his lambs, the bantam hens pecking at his shoetops and the wonderful mournful Highland cattle watching him from a distance, her attitude toward him shifted and swelled.

Part of the charm is his total lack of reticence. It makes up for her shy silences.

"One thing I remember," Andrew says. "Christ! I wish I could forget it, I drag it around like the mark of Cain, you know?"

Mary nods the requisite nod of empathy. In the dark of the car he hears rather than sees the gesture.

"He wasn't really an alcoholic, my dad, but he liked his Scotch whisky. Drinking made him pugnacious, it does that to our ethnic."

Meaning Scotch to the Scots, Mary thinks. She is descended from Calvinists and teetotalers, women who undress in the closet, men who wear nightshirts to bed, separate brooders.

"Sometimes he slapped us around when he'd taken a drop. Oh, not abusive, mind you, he always opened his hand to us, you see that, Mary?"

Mary sees a mailed fist and as it opens, fingers of bone. Ivory, perhaps. If it strikes, the fingers will shatter. *God punished you,* her mother says, over the cracked, distorted porcelain face of a doll.

"But this one time—God, how clear it all is to me! The three of us standing in the kitchen, and he hit her, he hit my mother full force across the face so hard that she staggered. Something caught fire in me, little kid that I was, nine or ten, and I grabbed up the bread knife and went for him screaming, 'Don't you ever touch her again, you son of a bitch,' that's what I screamed at him, and I went to waving the knife around like a demented thing. It wasn't very sharp, 'twas only fit for slicing warm bread; I remember thinking that inside my rage."

"But enough to scare him."

"Or bring him to his senses. He left off and stormed out the door. I don't remember the rest of that day. But next day, the humiliation of it, Mary, my mother made me apologize to him. Can you imagine? I had to say I was sorry, Da, for making such a swear. It was the son of a bitch, you see, more than the knife that upset her."

"Maybe she couldn't acknowledge the knife part," Mary suggests. "It was so scary maybe she had to pretend that part didn't happen."

"That's it!" Andrew exclaims; is he truly excited by this insight? "All these years I've been puzzling over it, it hurts me still, every time. Her siding with him after. But you know, there wasn't a mark on her, he'd opened his hand to her too. The man wasn't a batterer."

"Still," Mary says, dogged in her righteousness, "she was wrong to do that to you. It was cruel, it demeaned your manliness." Even knowing how she flatters him with her outrage. Even feeling the warm flush of sympathy for the boy locked inside as he takes her in his wide arms.

Sometimes when she catches sight of herself sideways in the mirror, then turns to confront her bones, the outline of her skull conveys the message of her death. Sometimes she broods that life has cheated her, that it has withheld much from her. But then, she reasons, she has not really met it halfway. She has gone only as far as she wanted. Although she longs for a child let down to her from heaven in a cloud, or washed up on this riverbank, she is not discontent with things as they are. It is a long way back to the arid, marginal land of her childhood, to the house of no books and few words.

The Highland steer, with their remarkable sheepdog faces and flat horns that stick out like immense misplaced mustaches, looked especially melancholy this evening on the hill against the setting sun. Mary thinks determinedly about the animals. What Andrew is doing, the way he gasps puts her in mind—again!—of the sheep thrown on their backs by her dad. And her struggling to clap the board in place. No wonder she invokes an image of the placid cattle while she strokes Andrew's damp back.

Duncan conjugates *venir*. He stumbles on *je viendrai*. Mary discusses the forms *venant* and *venu*. *Revenant* and *devenu*. Half the class dozes amiably in the overheated room. Even with the windows flung wide the air grows stale. The oxygen is used up, the radiators knock enthusiastically, everything drowses. The heating plant takes two days every spring to shut down. In autumn the process is reversed; everyone shivers hunched in multiple sweaters until the heating plant can catch up. Mary wonders if the school engineers ever plan ahead, ever listen to the long-range weather forecasts. Meanwhile, another drought-stricken summer is expected in Eureka. She is trying to avoid that last refuge on earth.

Que deviendra d'elle? What will become of her? she teaches her students. *C'est à devenir fou!* It's enough to drive one mad! She has them recite.

In Eureka, her father, diminished by drought and inflation, embittered by recession, grows more and more right-wing, a hawk seeking limited nuclear retaliation. The antinuclear rallies provide a useful focus for his paranoia. They don't want the power plants and they don't want to give up their outings or their toaster ovens, he says, and he is right. Fools, he calls them. Children wanting a cause, any cause to wave banners for. And he is right. Even while she agrees with him, even while she is overwhelmed by the enormity of the wrongs waiting to be set right, Mary knows she will go no further. Sometimes she thinks there is something in the soil of northern California, some anti-vitamin, that creates this inanition.

Once, her sister longed to be a librarian, to dress in skirts and walk about with clean manicured hands and stroke the bindings of old books. Now she is married to the electrician's son, a man as dry and uncompromising as the coastal

107

hills. Together they run a guesthouse on a side street in Mendocino, reserving the not-yet-restored third floor for themselves and their child. Mary thinks of Liza having to dress up every day during tourist season in a long skirt, having to play at pretend-frontierswoman in a massive Victorian house short of bathrooms. It is purgatory, getting the dress-up part of the wish. She thinks of the toddler kept on a leash and harness in the house to spare the antiques, the westering memorabilia necessary to establish the ambiance. What will become of her? Little, less, nothing at all.

When the term ends, Andrew and Amelia will be off to Bar Harbor to take up residence in their other home. The ancestral estate, Andrew calls it mockingly.

"A castle?"

"It's a bloody shoe factory, your cossill, four stories high and with all those square windows. Fit for the workers to look out of, big banks of windows, ugly as maggots under the tail." But it stands on the second cliff above the main peninsula. There are fourteen bedrooms, enough for all the assorted relations and houseguests.

"And the caretaker, he's the son of the son of the son who's looked after the place since 1902, when the great-great-grand-squire built it. I tell you, Mary. It's a blessing and a curse to marry into the robber baron's family."

Mary visualizes the departure. They will travel by caravan, four sons, two Corgis, two cats, rotating so that everyone gets to ride part of the way beside Andrew in the sports car. The rest of them will be wreaking havoc in the Travelvan, which Amelia will drive furiously and well with both her indoor-pale hands held high on the wheel.

Andrew and the boys will sail among the islands off the rocky Maine coast, taking all sorts of risks in bad weather and bragging about them afterwards. Andrew and the boys will picnic and frolic in the sun while Amelia makes notes in the margin of the first draft of her dissertation. And

Andrew and Amelia from time to time will give vast cocktail parties on the sand at the foot of their cliff, for which quantities of Polish vodka will have to be imported from Boston and conveyed down the steep slope on Andrew's and Duncan's and perhaps this year even Ian's shoulders.

Shortly before Labor Day, Andrew and Amelia will fly off to Cannes or Copenhagen or Capri. In these surroundings Amelia shades herself from the sun while Andrew's flushed face with his hectic cheeks turns frenetically toward this group and that, the insatiable party seeker.

When a poor boy marries well, he is the tail that wags the dog, the polestar to set sail by. For Amelia is a daughter of privilege. She stints at nothing. She does not shop in supermarkets or buy her clothes at discount houses in anonymous malls. She is never overlooked at parties; she never needs to balance her checkbook or even accommodate Andrew's desires. Amelia is toadied to wherever she goes; and although the knowledge of this does not make her miserable, it intensifies her natural reticence.

Mary does not even dislike Amelia. The two women are shy together. When Andrew is out of the room, they do not speak; they avoid eye contact. They tend to hum, pretending total absorption in whatever small task.

One day Amelia is restless. She has passed her orals as predicted; the dissertation looms. They talk about graduate school, a painful process for both. The difficulty is an equalizer.

Mary describes her terror of the language lab at night. Going down that corridor in a dank wooden building that had once been an army barrack.

"It creaked. Whether or not to footsteps. The only good things about the headphones was, with them on you couldn't hear any background noise. But I was too terrified to put them on for days."

"And too terrified not to," Amelia adds.

"Yes. And two years of that, parroting the exact sounds,

struggling to develop a decent accent on tape. God, my throat used to ache every night before I went to sleep, from rolling my r's."

And Mary describes her solitary six weeks in France, touring by bicycle, staying in youth hostels. She leaves out the small humiliations: the Italian man in her room in Marseilles, the bedbugs in Aix.

"I'm just a botch at languages," Amelia says. They are going to be friends shortly.

"It's like a musical ear," Mary says, mortified. "Everybody has something. I can't conceptualize at all in three dimensions."

They have tea together, Twining's Jasmine in fine porcelain cups that are in Amelia's family. It has a smoky aftertaste. Probably, Mary thinks, we will grow into one of those late-Victorian triangles, the middle-aged wife and the mistress, serving the separate needs of the gentleman-farmer-scholar.

The final week of school a crisis develops. The theology student and his wife who were to have looked after the livestock while Andrew and Amelia and the boys were away suddenly announce that they are separating. She is going back to her family in upstate New York. He is going to Mississippi to work in a clinic.

Mary, who has long thought she is waiting to meet her match, her ideal one, and has instead been locked into the daily grind of prep school life with the occasional visitor merely a perplexed father, sides with the wife.

Andrew, who loves peril and tests his whole lank strength against asphalt or ice, sides with the almost-minister.

Amelia, for whom men are nearly always treacherous, keeps her own counsel, but it is her idea to ask Mary to stay in place of the warring couple.

"I want this to be your real home, all summer," she says.

"And have your friends over," Andrew says with an expansive wave of his hand that dismisses the nonexistence of friends. "Give a barbecue, have a house party, have an orgy."

The departure is much as Mary has expected, except that they leave her the Corgis for company. She examines the two parental bedrooms, then chooses to sleep in Andrew's great soft featherbed. It is a nest, however lumpy. The dogs flop about on it, tongues lolling. No one comes to call except for United Parcel and a colleague of Amelia's who has misunderstood her departure date.

It is true that Mary has no friends; she has chosen not to cultivate any. Nevertheless, her life is full. Mornings, she translates some of the French poems Andrew has ferreted out for her from contemporary journals. Perhaps she can assemble a book this summer. Afternoons she wanders around the hundred-odd acres checking fences, looking for puffballs, and admiring the boundary oaks.

Once out in the pasture there is the contracted, baked smell of sun on earth, dry and cracked, where the passage of many feet has eroded the grass. At the bottom of the pasture runs a wide brook she longs to stand in, a brook wide enough to leave unfenced on the far side. Here and there the sheep have worn shallow gullies down to the water. Every so often an adventurous lamb roots out a place it seems safe to cross. If one wanders off or is swept downstream, another may follow. Andrew has warned her to watch for strays lest the neighbors' dogs get them.

She is to be on the lookout for lambs' testicles and tails. Best to pick them up and bury them in the lime pit Andrew has prepared behind the barn. Otherwise the rats get them and are emboldened to try for more. Rats can drag down a banty hen, even though the bantams are good fliers. Mary, who wants no deaths during her tenure, scrupulously polices the pasture each day.

And if the years pass this way and she has this small hold on Andrew, nothing more? If she is to teach the conjugations of *arriver* and *venir*, of *aller* and *voir* to Ian and Quentin in their turn, even to Douglas, and nothing more?

She will be like the all-black Dorset ram whose curled horns always put her in mind of the braids her mother used to wear, long ago, wound over her ears. The ram running free with the flock all summer, waiting for the ewes' estrus to come. Waiting for fall, to be of use.

The Town Records
Its Deaths

❧

Leopold Petrus fell over in his vegetable garden while he was gathering the zucchini glut. He was a sturdy, obese man, six feet tall. His bald head was dappled by a freckled sunburn. His blue eyes, the simple, direct blue of new marbles, stared upward in the full heat of the sun.

It was the rutting end of August. Overnight, the vines kept extruding new bulges which swelled by noon to individual fruits. Left to their own nature, these took cover under the spiny leaves and within a week had grown to grotesque proportions.

Poldi was famous in Lemford, Vermont, for his summer garden, which he tucked up each November under a four-inch blanket of horse manure. He preferred goose droppings as a more digestible top dressing, but he made do. In April while his plow blade still encountered jagged facets of ice, he turned the manure into the soil. And then he churned the whole mass even finer the first week in May, before he planted. The secret was in not planting too soon. The secret was energy, ego, and a willingness to get right down to weeding at the height of the mosquito season.

Lemford was celebrating its bicentennial the summer of Poldi's stroke. In spite of its weighty history, it was one of those towns where almost everyone had come from somewhere else. The original settlers have moved on to stone-free Ohio in the 1830s. The latter-day old-timers had sought out cities where jobs were to be had. Thus newcomers were hardly resented. After three or four years they became aldermen or got themselves appointed road agent and were absorbed into the body politic. Poldi, now in his ninth season as fenceviewer, had come to Lemford from his native canton of Graubunden in a generalized dispersion of Petruses in the twenties. There were cousins and courtesy cousins of his stationed all over Epworth County, a fine industrious overweight horde of them. Some were in capons, others in strawberries. One cousin had a prize flock of Toggenburg goats on his hilltop farm. They stripped the pasture and devoured the brush. The wind scoured the whole land bare in winter. It was appropriate, his own Alp.

When he was not settling boundary disputes in his official capacity, Poldi dabbled. He had been in pigs, beef cattle, turkeys, even snapdragons. Here and there he lost money; here and there he turned a profit. During the Depression he had bought up two thousand acres of scrub woodland for back taxes. From time to time he cut them over for the pine and lavished the cash on his doomed enterprise. Now he was a major landowner, someone to reckon with.

"Sometimes I think Poldi is a blessing I don't deserve," Franny Cotton would say. She said it the day he plucked a terrified barn swallow out of her living room curtains (she had been washing windows) and set it free outside. The summer the well went dry, Poldi descended with Hank

114

Cotton to shovel out the sludge that had blocked the underground spring. "He just came over," Hank marveled as Franny hosed them both with the newly restored spray. "He just came over to lend a hand."

The Cottons were Poldi's nearest neighbors. They were wiry, intense people, on the small side; physically, they could have been brother and sister. She had a luminous, slightly crooked smile. His face was kind, with deep crow's-feet and laugh lines. Seven years ago Hank and Franny had drawn a circle on a map within which, they had agreed, it would be feasible to drive back and forth for weekends. The grease pencil had gone through Lemford. There, on the dirt-road side of the river that bisected the town, they had found a house and barn in an advanced state of dereliction. The house sat back on a ridge between two rises, fronting only on more treetops, but if they had been able to cut a clear swath to the west, Poldi's house would have risen over their heads like a modest castle. From that angle, his trout pond would have formed the moat. Board fences, painted white, enclosed the fiefdom.

It came to pass, that first summer, that the Cottons' daughter, twelve-year-old Nina, pined for a pony. Specifically, she pined for a graceful but flighty Connemara named Deirdre whose owner was being taken at the whim of her parents to Europe. This particular pony must have not only a barn to sleep in but a paddock in which to roam about. The paddock must have three rails all around, high enough so that flighty Deirdre the Connemara would not think of leaping.

"My God," Poldi inquired mildly at the construction site, "what you gonna keep in there, Nina? Elephants?"

For this reason the Cottons' paddock had one six-foot-high side and three that were four feet high.

When it came to giving advice, Poldi had no contender. Ask him what size mesh would keep lambs penned, how to split the unsplittable elm logs, or how to bank a wood stove so the fire would last all night. He volunteered where the elderberries grew, the season for chanterelles and cêpes, how to pith a frog. He knew how to keep raccoons out of the corn patch with crumpled newspapers between the rows. "Coons won't come; they don't like the crackle their feet make." He knew how to catch the porcupine marauding on the willow. "Put out boards sprinkled with salt. Stay up late. When you hear your hedgehog out there," Poldi advised, "you go step on his tail, see? And club him like this!" A terrific overhead swipe with an imaginary sledge. "That way he never knows what hit him."

There had been a Mrs. Petrus—Agnes—dead many years. There was one son who had left Lemford for Columbia University and was now an investment counselor for a large Manhattan brokerage. The daughter-in-law was a painter. They had announced last spring, well before Poldi had set his zucchini seeds in the heavily manured soil, that they were having a baby. "If it's a boy they gonna name it Peter Ivan," Poldi said. "No reason. *Ivan*. They just like the way the names go together. If it's a girl, Ingrid. Ingrid, now, I can see that. It goes good."

Poldi hoped for a grandson even if it was to be named Peter Ivan. The sorrow of his and Agnes's life was that they had striven mightily and brought forth but an only child, a change-of-life baby. "A frost blossom," Poldi said. "Least they're starting sooner, maybe they gonna have lots of kids. Maybe with little kids they gonna want to give them some fresh air to breathe, they gonna visit me more."

They were standing in his kitchen. Franny and Nina and he. "I know what Nina here is thinking," he said, "but I'm hoping for a boy. I'm too old to change. A grandson is a monument."

And he served the raspberry pie, his specialty.

Nina had stood in the center of the thicket where the canes are thorniest and done the picking. She was a college freshman that year; what she now knew was that some things are worth overlooking. "Incredibly sexist," she murmured to Franny in the doorway, but maintained a policy of silence.

Poldi's desserts all began with a cup of butter and a cup of sugar creamed together. Eggs were then beaten in, and generous amounts of kirsch. The raspberries were merely the vehicle.

To live with such a neighbor at hand! The Cottons grew tranquil in the country, pointed their twin chimneys, repaired the split clapboards. They enlarged their vegetable garden and bought a freezer. Hank Cotton, fifty-two, in air conditioners and industrial refrigeration, began taking off Fridays to augment his weekends. He had grown up playing stoopball on West 72nd; now he knew the names of twenty trees. In World War II he had marched across North Africa guarding German PWs and eating sand. Now he had cross-country skis with all the right waxes. Although Nina had outgrown her fervor, in summer he leased two quiet horses from a stable in the valley and he and Franny rode up the back trail regularly, past the Petrus place, out to the elderberry preserve along the old beaver pond. He knew enough people to wave to; he studied the county area maps and learned the old names of what had once been neighborhoods and crossroads.

For Franny, Poldi Petrus was a particularly lustrous figure. While Hank had played stoopball and street hockey until it was too dark to follow the puck, she had spent her childhood at the piano. Her father would not take his children to the zoo for fear of exposing them to parasites or exotic inhalants. There were other outdoor terrors: traffic, muggers and rapists, pushers, winos, addicts. She was never unattended; still, there were days when she felt so depersonalized that she had to recite her name over and over to stay sane.

In the country Franny at first experienced a mild agoraphobia. So much sky! A bowlful of it, slopping over in all

117

directions. A silence that filled her ears with her own heart-beat. Unspecified dangers lurked. Something might be in those woods, around that bend in the path, lying flat out in the pasture grass, unseen. For a long time she busied herself with the house—safer indoors—cleaning, rearrang-ing, baking bread.

Then she discovered wild flowers, matching them to the handbook, and pursued them deeper into the woods. After that, it was edible plants and berries, followed by birds, birds' calls, and birds' nests. She was a methodical person, a list keeper, a noter of order and variety, of temperature differentials and the placement of chipmunk holes. Trea-sures she could not identify she took to Poldi.

"Canada goose feather," he would say. "Inky cap. May-apple. Oak gall." Each one was a signal for a reminiscence. "One year when the Canada geese were going over, on their way north, I looked out my back door and I saw this big cow trampling around in the dead cornstalks. So I grabbed up a neck rope and a broom. I was gonna shoo her off the garden, then halter and tie her till I could find the owner. I thought it was prob'ly something of Conover's; his cattle roamed because he never kept 'em watered.

"So there I am whacking away at this t'ing with the broom and it doesn't move. It doesn't back off like any cow I ever knew. Remember, it was awful early in the morning. Finally I look up, and I look into the face of this enormous bull moose."

Of mayapples, wistfully: "Agnes used to love them. She made a kind of pie, they're only good baked, you see. One year when I was out gathering her a basketful, up by Tin-gel's Corners, you know, I sat down against a tree to light my pipe. I was sitting there real still, like this, when a Canada lynx walked out of the woods. He was close to me as you are now, pale gray with whitish spots and tiny ears, but I was downwind to him; he didn't smell me. Lucky I didn't have my gun, he was too purty to shoot."

118

Hank doubted this story, as he preferred to doubt the numerous bear stories, he did not choose to believe in danger. The moose, which had happened even longer ago, he thought was allowable.

Nina took a week's leave from her summer job in a medical lab and came to Lemford for the bicentennial celebration. She had long dark hair that she braided or pulled back or wore up in a twist according to her mood. The braids were her family look. David, carefully described as a friend of Nina's who had graduated from med school and was about to begin his internship, came too.

It was not an altogether successful stay. Ever since his childhood in the Far East, David had been allergic to mosquito bites. Even though Lemford's insects were on the wane, he carried an ice cube around in a bit of paper towel at all times, leaving little puddles on the furniture. He never complained, simply pressed his red welts with the ice from time to time; thus Franny felt it would be ungenerous to mention the puddles.

Nina was in awe of David's mind and persisted in saying so. "He is a totally serious person," she insisted.

It turned out that David was an excellent horseman. He had grown up in Thailand and had learned how to ride at the Bangkok Polo Club among other privileged Western children whose fathers served in their countries' legations.

Hank mistrusted David, who spoke four languages and was rootless. This large, pink, blond young man with spaces between his teeth was not what he had intended for his daughter. Although they observed the decorum of separate rooms, Hank had the uneasy surety that David and Nina were living together in New York. Further, the young man never appeared at breakfast. He studied late, Nina defended. He had a different circadian rhythm, his day began at noon and spilled over well past midnight.

Hank said it was rude, in somebody else's house.

"That's terribly bourgeois," Nina said.

"Bourgeois is a house in the country," her father told her.

"No, really! It isn't fair. You disapprove of David because he has a different life-style, but you adore Poldi Petrus and *he* has an even weirder one."

"How, weirder?"

"Well, for one thing, he eats too much. His arteries are probably all *clogged* with whipped cream and butter and all those liver pâtés."

"The Swiss are all overweight," Franny said.

"But if David did it you'd call it self-indulgent. And talk about ethnic stereotypes! The Swiss are *not* all overweight."

"Okay. The Petruses are. It's genetic."

"And what about living alone up there, playing games with making a living? Snapdragons in this climate, for God's sake! And now he's going to breed *carp* in his pond."

"He is?" Franny was intrigued.

"That's what he said yesterday. Of course by this morning it may be miniature donkeys for all I know. Anyway, if it was anybody else, you'd be all *over* them yelling it was inconsistent or wasteful of their talents."

"He's an old man," Hank said patiently. "He grew up in another culture."

"David grew up in another culture."

"What," Hank asked, rising to a new level of exasperation, "has that got to do with it?"

"Face it, Pa. Everything."

On Saturday the Cottons and their houseguest took part in the commemorative parade. Everyone wore costumes. The Shriners' marching band, imported from Rockland and outfitted with purple fezzes, preceded them. David, bandaged in old sheets, riding bareback on Hank's gelding, received an Honorable Mention as a desert sheikh.

After the chicken barbecue and the cake sale, between sets of the square dance, they all wandered over to the Town Hall to purchase their copies of the Lemford Town History. Poldi was jubilant; his house, dating from the Revolutionary War, was prominently featured. The Cottons' house was not mentioned by name. Hank was disappointed to find it referred to as another "hillside farm in the Acre District dating back to the opening years of the nineteenth century."

The annals had been reverently prepared to incorporate much of the earlier history of the town, or as much as had been preserved in the chronological records. It was David who pre-empted the book and sat curled up in Hank's favorite armchair the next day reading bits and pieces aloud to them.

"Hey, Neen, listen to this! 'In the summer of 1816 on inauguration day in June it snowed to the depth of four inches. Not a month in the entire year escaped the frost.' "

Franny murmured sympathetic interest. Actually, she was fascinated but would have preferred finding the item for herself.

"Grasshoppers!" David said. " 'In 1826 Lemford was inundated with a plague of grasshoppers such as had never been noted before.' "

"Locusts," Nina said knowledgeably. "Don't you remember Poldi talking about the locusts. How they ate their way through his pine grove the first year when he was raising Christmas trees?"

"Not in 1826."

"Maybe in 1926, though."

"And how about this little item? Did you know that when the railroad opened in 1849 they imported an elephant for the occasion? 'It was the first time an elephant set foot in Lemford.' "

Meanwhile, Poldi lay unconscious among the zucchinis.

He was not discovered until late afternoon when Hank, escaping David's relentless narration, decided to return an extension ladder. A wheelbarrow full of grass clippings stood at the edge of the garden.

He was retelling it at dinner.

"I knew something was wrong. I knew he wouldn't have left the barrow like that."

"Pulse was thready," David reported, for Hank had called the State Police barracks and then, while waiting, the medical student. "His breathing was shallow, probably an embolism. We couldn't do much until they got there with the oxygen. He came to, though, while we were lifting him."

It was Nina who wept. "I can't help it," she hiccuped. "I mean, there he was telling those stories, bragging all the time about bringing home the dead elk or bobcat or whatever. And now it's like . . . they've taken his gun away. They've taken away his hunting knife and his ax and his trousers."

Franny went into the hospital in Brattleboro twice a week to see him. Some Sundays she and Hank went together. Early in October, just after the first hard frost, Poldi was swaddled in white and brought home. A middle-aged cousin and wife and wife's sister moved in to look after him, and a steady procession of Petrus relatives came to call.

And then, surprisingly, Nina and David turned up for the weekend.

"Columbus's birthday! Hail Columbus!" Nina cheered.

It was Indian summer. The woods were radiant. Thus she and Franny walked up the dusty beaten path to visit Poldi in the little kingdom to the west. From the edge of his trout pond, they stood looking down. The trees had cast many of their leaves. Below, the tin roof of their own barn winked in the sunlight.

"I remember this used to seem so far when I was a little kid," Nina said.

"You weren't so little. You were twelve."

"Yeah, well, twelve is funny. Remember that Connemara pony? I used to ride up through here to get to the Plains Road and I used to be terrified, practically paralyzed with fear, till we got out in the open, till we got to this field."

"You were? What were you afraid of?"

"Poldi's bears, the ones he was always claiming he saw or scared off or got a shot at."

Franny squeezed her shoulder. "Poor babe! How could you know what a handsome liar he was!"

"Well, I knew and I didn't know, sort of."

"It's like a wake with a living corpse," Nina described to David when they came heavily home. "I mean, he's propped up there in a wheelchair with shawls, he can't speak, really, but he makes sounds that are supposed to be speech."

"He's aphasic," David prompted.

"Yes. And all around him the family is taking turns telling his old stories, what I used to call his yesteryear stories."

"Like what?"

"Well, Cousin William told this long one about a bachelor hunting trip back in the thirties. It seems that he and four or five other men and Poldi all came up for the deer season. Poldi stayed at the house, since he was the host, to clean out the flues and get the fires going and start supper, and the rest of them all fanned out. Finally, around five o'clock just before it got dark he went out alone and walked up on the ridge, our ridge here. Well, *you* know. Poldi took exactly one shot and he got the only deer of the entire hunting trip."

"And how does he react?"

"That's the *point*, David. They're telling these stories and they keep looking over at him for confirmation and nodding, and there he is, entirely expressionless."

"If he hasn't shown more improvement than this by now," David said, "chances are he won't change very much. Stroke cases like this, the first six weeks are the crucial ones."

"Mr. Know-it-all," Nina said.

"Let's hope you're wrong," Hank said, straightening up from the hearth where he had been tinkering with the fire. "Anyway, he's a grandfather now. They had a little girl last week, his son and his wife."

"Ingrid," Nina remembered.

"Ingrid," Franny agreed. "Eight pounds, eleven ounces, bald as an onion. But no one knows whether Poldi understood or not. They told him, they tell him all sorts of things, they give him a daily report as if he were just deaf or blind, but there's no way to see on his face whether it gets through."

"I wish he were dead!" Nina said. "What a rotten deal, not to let him die! I wish you'd never found him, Pa!"

"But we don't know, babe," Hank said gently.

"We know enough!"

But David had found the history book and had settled in again in the overstuffed armchair. "This is priceless, Neen! Listen to this and see if you don't think it has biblical overtones. Doesn't this sound like something out of First and Second Kings? 'Martin Ackworth of Acre bled to death in the woods in 1809 from a cut in the foot.' 'In 1851 Miss Patience Thatcher was run over and killed by a train of cars at Rockmer.' 'Bartlett Benton, an insane man, lost his life in a house that was consumed by fire in 1800.' 'Asa Hodges was killed by a falling tree, and a child of Whitcomb Evert got a fresh-shelled bean in its throat and choked to death in its mother's arms.' "

Hank made an impatient sound in his throat and left the room.

" 'Jonathon Daniel was thrown from the tongue under the wheel of a loaded cart and killed in 1820, while Mrs. Begley, the second wife of Abner, threw herself into the well. . . .' What's the matter with him?"

"He thinks what you are doing is prurient," Franny said clearly.

"What am I doing?"

"You don't know, do you?" Nina asked. "To you it's just something in a book, something like an anatomy drawing."

"*Neen.* I'm reading you as it is written."

"You are cheapening the past by going at it like a voyeur," she said.

"What are you talking about?"

"Like a goddam Peeping Tom. You haven't earned the right to mock the dead."

"Mock the dead?"

But she had already left the room.

Neither Franny, chopping cabbage for coleslaw, nor Nina, now splitting logs out in the woodshed, had told it all. That afternoon, Poldi had been wheeled back to his bedroom, lifted hydraulically to his electrically operated hospital bed, tended by his womenfolk. Franny and Nina had put their heads in at the door to say goodbye and he made two little arm strokes, inward ones, the kind that beckon. Both hesitated, thinking he had wanted to wave goodbye, but he repeated the movements urgently. They crossed to the bed. Franny a little ahead. He lifted the one functioning hand, pointed it at her chest, then drew it twice across his own throat. She recoiled. What she couldn't forgive in herself was that she had recoiled. A child might choke meaninglessly to death on a bean. An unhappy wife could fling herself down a well. Why was Poldi Petrus, age seventy-two, required to go on?

Thanksgiving week Leopold Petrus died in his sleep. He was buried in the new extension of the Lemford cemetery, the third citizen of Epworth county to be laid to rest since the addition had been opened. His death was duly recorded.

The Missing Person

They leave the car at one of those park-and-lock lots: NO ATTENDANT AFTER 7 P.M., the signs warn. But Alan says it is senseless to try to drive into center city at this hour and she agrees with him. She tucks her purse out of sight under the front seat, unwilling to carry it in the predictable crowd.

"You have to take something, Ellie, your wallet at least. You can't walk around the city like an orphan."

Because it is a very small fold-over wallet she argues only briefly, then thrusts it deep in her coat pocket. They trudge through blackened slush to the subway entrance.

Years ago, Alan lived here, a student at the university. He knows intersections, sirens, one-way streets; he is a confident, serious man. She has ridden the subway four times in her life. She is terrified but says nothing. Her terror, she knows, is banal. They are sucked into the tube; the sound presses against her ears. Alan's lips move. She nods, pretending to understand. At home it is so quiet she can hear the dog sneeze in the night. They are expelled at the correct stop.

Downtown is cluttered with Christmas lights and after-work pedestrians pushing in and out of shops. The corner taverns give off enough surplus heat to melt the sidewalks in rough arcs around their entrances. She comments on this, thinking of the sullen, now-empty wood stoves at home and their acres of forested, uninhabited land now locked under this new all-day snow.

They had driven 370 miles for this evening. They know no one in the city any more, except for Kathleen, their daughter-in-law, who has a part in the repertory production they have come to see. It is a substantial part, she has assured them by mail, the letter containing a pair of tickets. Kathleen still writes dutifully every six or eight months. She is living with an older man, a lighting technician. When the theater is dark she waits on tables in a nearby bistro. Words like co-vivant and psyche, life-style and energy bedeck her letters. Reading them, Alan snorts like a choosy horse picking through weeds for the timothy.

They are the parents of an MIA who married this girl six years ago on brief acquaintance. They feel wary about her still; her grief was shallow and impossible to sustain. Theirs is eternal.

James Alan, the son—Jay, they always called him—toyed with Canada, Sweden, and jail, but in the end inanition prevailed. He was drafted. He put on his country's uniform, he was written up in the *Argus County Gazette* under his high school graduation photo, and he came home on furlough that summer. Ellie remembers that his hands shook as if with cold. They were both ashamed of their fears, mother and son, sharing an aversion to Ferris wheels, observation towers, and diving boards, and they did not speak of his condition. Toward the end of the fourteen days he sent for Kathleen. They had been secretly married three months ago, he hoped his parents would love her as much as he did. His earnest face cracked with the desire to make an amalgam of his people, to consolidate his loyalties.

Kathleen wears her long hair parted in the middle. Whenever she leans forward it sweeps across her eyes, the corners of her mouth; an impediment, Ellie thinks. Kathleen loves bathrobes and long-sleeved shirts. When Jay's furlough ends, she takes with her his flannel, his chamois, and his royal-blue corduroy shirts to keep her warm all winter. Only two months later, before the weather has turned properly cold, he disappears in a helicopter, this child who dreaded heights.

Every year thousands of Americans die accidental deaths. Bizarre deaths, drownings, freak electrocutions, mushroom poisonings. A man chokes to death on a piece of steak in an expensive restaurant. A young woman falls from her loved and trusted horse and breaks her neck. Jay vanishes over hostile territory; neither he nor his eleven companions are ever found. When an only child leaves you—she cannot yet say dies—the air comes out of the basketball, the tire flattens, your own lungs threaten to crumple.

She is reclusive. She grows things, she preserves and freezes and dries them, she knows all the local wild mushrooms, all the local nuts. In the winter in her greenhouse she harvests cherry tomatoes and actual curly lettuce. Her project this year is to make Belgian endive sprout under layers of well-manured sawdust in boxes in the cellar. When she is not forced away from the farm, she is peeking under the sawdust to see if the roots have sent up any new growth yet.

This is the way Ellie's mind skips and bumbles as they gruel through the wet, half-hearted snowfall toward Liberty Street. They walk a little apart, husband and wife of twenty-eight years, not at all like two people who imagine they are holding one another. Ellie examines oncoming pedestrians. She notes what they are wearing, how they

129

walk. A city stride is tight, she is thinking; at the same time she is thinking her winter coat is years behind the style. People walk angrily with tense buttock muscles, probably from the hard sidewalk.

The light changes. She stands obediently on the curb, watching, mooning. When the green goes on, she starts across. Alan is not at her side. She stops, waiting for him to catch up; she steps out of the human flow and waits next to a building. The texture of the rough brick makes itself felt against her back as she tries to relax, to lean into and imprison the moment.

In perhaps ten seconds she is flooded with panic. He has been struck by a car, he has been mugged and dragged into an alley, he has suffered a stroke, a heart attack. She rushes back across the street, darting this way and that, like a dog separated from its master. Everything around her is normal. People press forward in both directions; they know what they are doing. Her ears are ringing, her eyes are filling with brilliant asterisks, her peripheral vision is fading.

A policeman was directing traffic at a major intersection two blocks behind her; she remembers passing him, re- members noting his cheeks inflated like birthday balloons around the whistle. He does not stop shrilling air through the whistle. Nor can she now attract his attention, even standing at his side, even tugging his sleeve. She is out of breath. It requires a great effort to remain coherent.

When finally he allots her a sentence—expecting, un- doubtedly, to be asked directions—he shakes his head de- cisively. He is Traffic, he shouts, and points where she must go. At the precinct house, two blocks west, three south, a patrol car is drawn up to the sidewalk. An altercation is taking place on the steps. There are raised nightsticks, grunts, a scuffle, arms pinned behind backs. She waits as long as she dares, watching the gray snowflakes melt as they strike pavement, enlarging the puddles like a late spring snow in the sugarbush.

Alan sells debarkers and wood chippers and other mechanical wood-harvesting aids. He can tell every species of tree from its bark and he can do this even with his eyes closed, just from the texture and aroma of the bark. Now he is getting into machinery that mills wood flour. Do you know about wood flour? she asks the sergeant. It's an expanding market, they add it to plastic as a low-grade reinforcement. It's dangerous, it's explosive, a spark will set it off. I always thought if something happened to Alan it would be with wood flour.

She realizes she is babbling. The sergeant scribbles as she talks. Probably he thinks she is part of an underground cell, part of a plot to blow up the city's water supply. Meanwhile in the back room she is aware of a methodical thumping, muffled voices. A suspect is being beaten? Someone is cranking a mimeo machine? It is hard to concentrate, she feels scattered. She feels as though the top of her head might come off and her brains ooze out, all gray and clayey.

Her husband might have stepped out to visit a friend, the sergeant suggests. Or he might have stepped in somewhere to answer a call of nature. Has she continued on to the theater where, after their accidental separation, he is possibly now anxiously waiting for her to catch up with him?

She has not. In any case, he has the tickets.

Has she thought of returning to the parking lot to see if he is waiting at the car for her, having become accidentally separated from her and realizing that she might grow confused about the location of the theater but remember where they have parked the car?

No, she has not thought of that. Besides, he has the car keys. Hers are in her purse. Which is locked in the car.

Any history of mental disorder?

Wordlessly she shakes her head.

Maybe—this hangs on the air although it is not actually voiced—maybe he has grown tired of her and has elected this admittedly uncommon method of deserting her. Does she remember any unusual incident that transpired between them today?

She resolves not to mention the incident of the wallet. After all, Alan is practical. She ought not to wander around a big city without her name and address and a few dollars. This is not Argus County where the doors of households are left open and only stall latches are shut. No, nothing. Nothing!

Hundreds of people are reported missing every day, it is explained to her patiently, but with an air of lassitude. Of every hundred persons who are reported missing by their loved ones, 99 and 99/100ths of them are deliberately missing. They have dropped out, taken a powder, vamoosed, they don't want to be found. And 99 percent of the 99 and 99/100ths undergo a change of heart within the first twenty-four hours. They get over their bad feeling, they experience remorse, they return. This is the reason for the Police Department's regulation. A missing persons bulletin cannot be issued on her husband until approximately this time tomorrow.

No, he is genuinely sorry, he is not empowered to take down a description of the—ah, possibly missing person until tomorrow evening at approximately . . .

She gets up finally, fumbling, realizing that she is not carrying the pocketbook a woman may fumble to retrieve from her lap as she rises. She has no will. She is directionless. She cannot see beyond the passage of twenty-four hours so that she may return to this varnished brown office and describe her vanished husband to an officer of the law. For surely if they know what he looks like, they can find him?

Gradually her mind refocuses on the theater. It is all up to Kathleen now. It soothes her to imagine that Alan and Kathleen have been in secret communication all along. There is a word for it, it will come to her, right now she must just concentrate on walking in the right direction. Back, back past the traffic cop, his whistle now dangling on his chest. Alan knows how she feels about Kathleen. She pretends she is indifferent to her, but in truth she has resented her from the beginning. Back down Liberty Street in the direction of the theater, which actually is housed in a former church. That much she remembers from Kathleen's letter. The word is *collusion*.

The church is shabby inside. It smells of mildew and low-grade heating oil. Footpaths are worn in the maroon carpet. The lobby is deserted except for a slender young man in a blue jumpsuit. The ebb and flow of conversation come through the double doors; stagey laughter follows. The play is in progress. She and the young man converse in hushed tones. He has a pale goatee which points at her as he talks. Everything is haloed in her sight. Her words have little haloes around them too, little sunbursts of Indian decoration.

She does not have the tickets, she is explaining; they are complimentary tickets sent to her and her husband. Who is—she does not know. By Kathleen Blakeslee. She is proud to have remembered Kathleen's other name. Their daughter-in-law.

What a shame, murmurs Narrow Beard, because Kathleen was called out of town just this morning. It seems her father had a heart attack in Cincinnati. Her part for this performance is being played by Angela Rountree.

They stand silently side by side, equally passive, although he is imparting information and she is absorbing it, her mind racing, seizing on, discarding, possibilities. There is the scattered affirmative sound of applause. Lights go up, the double doors open.

"Excuse me," her companion says, distracted. He has his duties to perform. She stands for a moment watching the audience file past as if magically Alan and Kathleen might appear among them. Finally, she joins the last little cluster of people moving out into the night. As if she too had a sense of purpose, trailing behind a young couple, walking east again through the still intermittent snow to the mouth of the subway.

She is absorbed once again into the tunnel. Fishing out change for a token, she thinks to count her money: $21.39. Strange, that extra ten, she has no memory of it. Somewhere Alan asked her to make change, somewhere in a turnpike Howard Johnson's handed her a ten-dollar bill and asked? She has no memory. Terrible at figures, at maps, at mechanical devices. Intuitive. Adept with hammer and saw, nonmotorized tools, calm with animals. That's who I am, she tells herself over and over as the subway lights slap past, riffling like cards in a deck, and the clatter of a train passing in the other direction assaults her ears. Who I am Iam miam. She gets off at the correct stop, she is followed. Deliberately she slows down, listening. She waits to be mugged. They are her own footsteps. She finds herself on the correct street, at the next corner looms the park-and-lock, lights around the perimeter feebly gleaming.

Somewhere toward the third section over, she thinks. Just below the middle strip. Here and there a set of headlights goes on, a motor makes that reassuring cough as it turns over. Others too are wholesomely bent on retrieving their cars. She does not tell herself that Alan waits inside theirs, she is beyond such fantasies now. There is a spare key attached by magnet under the left rocker panel; if only she can get inside! They took this step a year ago when Alan absentmindedly locked the keys in the car at the Eastern States Exposition. They are anomalies, both of them, unused to locks.

But the car is not where she remembers it. Not in the next row or the next. Frantic now, reversing sides, she prowls up and down the rows. Two figures are sitting on the hood of an old Edsel watching her. There is the glint of a bottle being passed between them, and by its glint, as it were, she spots her car—it is *her* car now—parked right next to the Edsel.

They face each other, she and the two men. Boys, really. One is reed-thin with a shaved head the shape of a football. A religious sect? she thinks. An escaped convict? The other, heavier, bobs around. He is less clear, wrapped in an oversize coat; no, a blanket. They are black.

She cannot require herself to kneel down, feel under the car for the key. She cannot take possession of her car in their presence. The menace is so direct that someone, she thinks, has told them where to wait. Her plan is known. She will not invite a blow on the head with a blunt instrument, she will not so easily become another victim to the city. She moves away, giving no sign, as if still in search of a car, walks farther and farther, does not turn until she knows she is out of sight. And watches the two forms asprawl on the hood of the Edsel in the snow and the bottle tilting up.

Somehow, she has no recollection of the entrance or the stairwell or even of the station platform, she is in the subway again. In motion, this time she leans her head back against the metal frame of the car, letting the pulse of the underground rock her. The shrieks of the rails, the protests of metal on metal blur into a kind of dangerous music. It is the music of the sea. Washed overboard, she bobs on the surface, determined not to drown. She does not even know which direction she is going in. She has not looked at any of her traveling companions to sort out the indigent, the malicious, and the crazy. At the end of the line only one other person is left in the car, a tired-looking middle-aged woman dressed in men's sneakers and wearing a bandanna knotted under her chin. When they get out, Ellie walks as close to this woman as she dares. Although they do not speak, there is something hovering between them. They are allies.

Suddenly she realizes how tenuous the thread that ties her to the parking lot, the car, her pocketbook within, her identity. The subway has become her connector; she turns and hurries back down the dank stairs. Conveniently, at the end of the line there is no choice to make. Conveniently, a car yawns in the station. A guard lounges alongside the empty conveyance. He blows his nose onto the tracks and she is grateful to him. She enters the car and goes immediately to the map to find her stop. Luckily, it is the name also of a famous painter and she has no difficulty locating it. Fourteen stops, though. She has come a long way. She sits down opposite the map so she can keep an eye on it. The car starts up.

It is after midnight now, the streets on the outskirts deserted, the sidewalks coated with a thin grease of city snow. Approaching the parking lot she has to fight her terror; suppose those two men are still there? She has to fight an impulse to fall to her knees, to wriggle along unseen like a guerrilla between the rows.

The Edsel is gone. Snow is beginning to stick to the wet lozenge of asphalt it covered. She can hear her heart. It makes explosive thumps of relief in her ears. Now she falls to her knees, groping under the car for the little magnetic cup. Her hand fastens on it immediately. What luck! She withdraws the key.

She opens the door and drops onto the front seat, has barely the presence of mind to pull the door closed and press down the lock before great waves of trembling overtake her. It is a shivering fit, the kind she endured during frequent childhood bouts of fever. Her body trembles, chattering like aspen leaves in a light wind. From time to time the quaking subsides. She takes a cautious calming breath as one does after the hiccups. Two breaths, three; then some subliminal thought racks her anew with tremors.

Little by little she sleeps, shakes, sleeps again. When she comes fully awake there is a line of light in the sky and her purse lies heavy in her lap like a cold animal. Somehow she has pulled it out from under the seat. She recognizes that she has been hugging it.

As soon as it is light enough to navigate without head-lights, she takes out her own set of car keys and eases out of the lot. Except for the trucks, there is no traffic on the main artery into center city. Despite her normal panic at the multiple signs full of proscriptions, she has no trou-ble finding Liberty Street. After Liberty Street, the pre-cinct house.

A new sergeant is on duty. It has not occurred to her that last night's man is off duty, has gone home for break-fast, is already safely asleep. She is surprised by her anger. This morning's sergeant respects her account of the night that has passed. He notes down carefully a description of Alan. She gives him a snapshot from her wallet, four years old, but accurate enough. In it, Alan stands by the barn, stiffly posed, squinting into the sun. The head of one horse, the rump of another are visible on the left. Alan is holding a sledge. He looks boyish and capable. And most of all, he looks startlingly like Jay.

Finally, she begins the long drive home. Oddly peaceful, she ascribes the serenity to her extreme fatigue. Also to shock. You're in shock, she tells herself sternly, waiting to grieve. Think how you miss him. Think how you love, loved him.

But she cannot. The main thing now, the thing that is flooding her with euphoria, is how she has survived her ordeal. How she has coped. She has conquered the subway. She has forced the city to declare Alan a Missing Person twelve hours ahead of schedule. She knows now that Jay has been dead all these years. When will she need to know about Alan? She reviews the extreme and contradictory emotions the sight of Alan's dead, well-known body will arouse in her.

Resolutely, holding to fifty-five mph on the hypnotic turnpike, she pulls the lumpy brown leather pocketbook onto her lap and rests her free hand, palm down, on its surface.

West

It is morning. After Lena has stripped Marigold's udder and strained the goat's milk into the refrigerator jug; after she has fed the horses and the dogs and shooed Evvie's gander off the lawn to the edge of the fire pond and scattered a handful of grain there to keep him interested, she goes to the little one-room building where Evvie lives. The building housed a generator once, before the county brought power up the hill. This improvement took place after World War II, the war Lena's dead husband used to call the Biggun, as if it had been a hurricane or World Series game. Now the cabin holds a young woman—a sort of flower child, Lena thinks—who takes her cats to bed. Sometimes her electric-guitar-playing lover stops by. He is allergic to cat hair. If Lena looks out in the morning and sees the two cats mooning around stalking chipmunks, she knows Malcolm is visiting.

Evvie is supposed to help out around the place summers in return for room and board. In common with her generation, she has a remarkable capacity for sleep. To sleep late, sleep through, fall asleep, stay asleep, sleep in the day-time—all these enviable talents Lena has lost.

Evvie goes barefoot. She bakes bread with no additives, she rinses alfalfa sprouts and keeps them in dark places in jars. Naked to the waist, she mows the lawn. Barefoot she goes into the pasture to fetch the horses, her thick defiant hair bounding on her shoulders. Sometimes Lena braids it for her in one wide plait down her back and Evvie complains with each tug.

"It's too tight. It's giving me a headache."

"Stand still," Lena says automatically. She is back braiding the hair of her daughters. "Your part is crooked. Did you comb this mop at all? Stand still."

On her days off Evvie hitchhikes into Portland as if the world were good and all cars were in the possession of kind, mannerly people. Still, no harm befalls her. Whereas Lena's younger daughter, Nell, working for a UN agency that resettles refugees in Uganda, has not been heard from in six weeks. Top officials in Geneva say it is not safe to assume anything. Neither assume that she is alive and well in the bush, far from roads, postal services, or phones, nor that she has been ambushed, raped, butchered.

"So what you're saying is, it is safe to assume it is not safe," Lena says, long distance into the telephone. She uses a dangerous, controlled tone that lies just this side of hysteria.

"Neither the one thing nor the other," the dry voice repeats in a British English. It says *neither* with a long i.

That conversation took place a week ago. Lena concentrates on keeping going. Like most grown women, she has had considerable practice.

She has to rap really hard to break through the curtain that sleep has hung between Evvie and the day.

"You don't want roast goose, you better get out here and take charge of Jeeper." It is Lena's standard threat.

"Spinach soufflé, *caca d'oie* all over the lawn again, Evvie. *Toujours*, dammit."

Jeeper is the gander. Evvie is attached to the word; it was the first word she said, seventeen years before, when she and her mother had a working relationship.

"You mean you don't talk to each other?" Lena asked her once.

"Oh, we talk, all right. We just don't communicate."

"Tie him," Lena says, safe in the knowledge birds cannot be tied. "Do something, then. Make him a pen."

Lena can put up with almost anything in the animal department except poultry. She does not trust the bird around her grandson Joshua, who is six and wants to hug Jeeper. Joshua, her older daughter's child, visits every August. He likes living with Lena so much that he is staying through September this year for the Fall Foliage Festival. He is going to be in the parade!

Each autumn, with a parade and a fair, the town of Ramawa celebrates the phenomenon of the leaves turning. City people from as far away as Boston and Providence drive up for the day. They all wear their cameras, they stand in polite lines for the chicken barbecue, they buy up the local crafts and the dregs of the previous summer's antiques. The Farmers Market unloads bushels of apples and several varieties of squash. Pyramids of pumpkins diminish rapidly. The glint of money excites the community. The town fathers talk about a new police cruiser, about getting the road grader repaired.

Evvie's parents are prominent citizens of this town. Her father owns both the piano and crutch factories. The latter admittedly is a dying industry; aluminum prostheses are doing it in. Nevertheless, his workers still set ash, birch, and maple to soak, bending them to their supportive uses. Lena has a cutting board made of tag ends from the crutch materials. Warren G. Harding Morrison, an itinerant carpenter who rode across Kansas in the U.S. Cavalry in 1934

141

and rebuilt Lena's back porch in 1962, made it for her. It was a Christmas present the last winter he spent in Maine.

Evvie's father also owns the town's sand and gravel pits. It is his credo or boast that he takes care of His Men. When a fire wipes out the dreadful shanty three generations of Riggses have inhabited, Evvie's father directs the building of a new cottage. He installs the first indoor toilet in the history of the Riggses. Evvie's father routinely puts up bail money for His Men when they get drunk during the last of hunting season; frustrated from not having brought down their deer, they tear up the town. He sends the really sick to his own doctor and fires the malingerers. Hot noon meals are served to him. Women, he believes, are meant to prepare these.

Evvie, with her seeds and nuts and soymeal grains, is in retreat from his benevolent tyranny. Evvie's father is a good person; the town depends on him.

Evvie's mother always has the best float in the Fall Foliage Festival parade. She has won Best Float for ten years running. No one thinks seriously of competing against her. She borrows—seizes, actually—something motorized and strong from the piano factory or gravel pit garage two weeks before the parade. She incarcerates the forklift, dump truck, or backhoe in her driveway while layering it with bunting or crepe paper, purple-dyed cheesecloth, boughs of autumn leaves. Evvie's mother tends toward the simpler statements of patriotism: Pilgrim Fathers; Betsy Ross sewing the flag; the first Thanksgiving, complete with Indians.

"You know what would make her the happiest woman in the world?" Evvie says.

"What?"

"If she could be float-maker adviser to the Rose Bowl Parade. She'd die a happy woman."

Evvie wants to be Lady Godiva in the parade. Lady Godiva in a flesh-colored body stocking, her electric hair flowing loosely around the stocking. It's a protest against taxes, she has read somewhere. She wants to ride bareback on Doc, Lena's peaceful Palomino. Doc, who does as little as possible, is about to be pressed into service behind the high school brass band in the parade.

Fortunately, Lena thinks, animals are not able to anticipate. Doc is eating the late ladino clover, the last before September frosts turn it all to straw. Frost comes early along the midsection of the Maine coast, the growing season is woefully short. In summer the mosquitoes attain mythic proportions.

The reason Lena lives here at all, she will tell you, is inertia. Ten years ago, after her husband was killed swerving his station wagon to avoid a deer on the Maine Turnpike and striking instead a concrete abutment, she came back here to stay. This farmhouse had been their summer place, site of their best times. Nell and Joshua's mother, Rebecca, had already left home by then. The sense of how it had been gives Lena the courage yet again to get on with resisting changing it. The four horses, including the now aged gelding her husband used to ride, stay put in pasture and barn. She takes them out in rotation or enlists neighbors' children to ride with her. There is the harvest, enough produce to fill the freezer, and after that, the bone-jolting frosts, and then the snows. A long time of shoveling out to the barn to feed. A long slow time of protracted twilights, gray mornings. She does her grieving in solitary in the dark, mourning the absent daughters as much as the so-suddenly removed husband. What a strange procedure, to raise another woman! How different, how much the same her daughters' lives and hers!

It would fill a book, Lena thinks, trying to reconstruct how it is. Evvie takes up some of the empty space. Joshua is a brilliant migratory bird. Lena's house overflows with handbooks on herbs and ferns, wild-flower texts, small press collections of poems. She reads sociobiology, anthropology, natural foods cookbooks, African folk tales. There is time for the back issues of all the magazines the Ramawa Library subscribes to.

Little by little Lena has become an accepted Ramawan. In winter Evvie's father sends one of His Men up to check on her wood supply, her state of mind and body, the battery in her Jeep. When the first green shoots arrive in spring her nearest neighbor, a lobsterman's widow, walks up to gather fiddleheads.

Now that Joshua has entered her life, Lena gets to do some cosseting. She writes stories for him, she takes him to pick blueberries and catch butterflies. She gives him A plus in spying out puffballs. Next year she will find him the perfect pony. This year he will be in the parade.

But this is not an idyll. Loneliness enters in, days pass without exchange of human speech. Lena has some arthritis. She commences every day hurting. Cold weather makes it worse. Summers, unless the onshore breeze reaches into the hills, the deerflies bite cruelly. Joshua's parents have separated, Rebecca has had an abortion. With Nell first in New York, then in Geneva, training to go into the field— here Lena has a vision of vast dry meadows—the phone bill equals that from the Ramawa General Store. During periods of crisis the sisters call each other day and night. The mother calls the daughters, who tell her not quite what they tell each other. The daughters call the mother; then they must check back with each other. All the anguish and tenderness of these phone calls, all the complexity and caring of these relationships is lost forever in an age when nothing personal is written down. What a pity, Lena thinks, that no one is recording this oral history for a Ph.D. project.

The *New York Times* arrives in Lena's mailbox a day late. She follows events in the Third World, so far as they are reported. Before this assignment, Nell has worked in Haiti, in Recife, even in Sri Lanka. Mail has been spotty.

Letters that are written come, scattershot, out of sequence. The pale-blue feathery envelopes accumulate three and four deep; some letters are never delivered. The quality of the six-week silence is only more ominous, Lena tells herself, because Idi Amin has been missing, reportedly sighted here and there in the countryside with his last-ditch followers. A week later he is said to be elsewhere, hiding perhaps in Libya.

Libya, Lena says to herself. Togo, Niger, Mali, Burundi. She says the words under her breath, but nothing takes shape in her head. It is not like whispering Michigan, Minnesota, Florida, and seeing instant lakes, coastlines. Nevertheless, somewhere in Uganda at this moment a woman Lena's age is milking a goat. Into the cool, late September sky comes an African sun, fierce on the veldt, stinging the back of Lena's neck.

Evvie usually does the evening milking. Marigold jumps onto the platform in the barn and puts her head through the stocks so that she can reach her pail of sweet feed, a mix of grains made sticky with molasses. Joshua is waiting with a plastic saucer. He is going to feed the barn cats, two grown toms who disdain milk and stalk Joshua from the ledges around the tops of the horses' stalls.

" 'Michael, row your boat ashore. . . .' " Evvie sings pressing her head against Marigold's accommodating flank.

"Me too, Evvie," Joshua implores. She changes the song to "Joshie, row your boat ashore," and the child chimes in on the hallelu.

Tonight Lena and Evvie will finish the costumes for tomorrow's parade. Joshua's will be laced together with rawhide shoelaces borrowed from Lena's winter work boots. He will be a child of the Westward Movement. Parade watchers will know this. Everything, except the dark hole of Nell's absence, is explicable.

Memory gets things all wrong, Lena thinks, reviewing

145

whole patches of Nell's life, season by season. In one frame Nell is in the kitchen skimming the great boiling froth of strawberries for jam. She saves the scum in a soup bowl; both she and Lena love it stirred into yogurt. She is climbing back from the mailbox at the foot of the hill, vulnerable, unseeing, yet dodging stones and little pyramids of horse manure as she walks, reading a letter. One letter is an occasion for tears. As Lena, traitorous, watches from the front window, Nell stuffs the pages in her back pocket, blows her nose, enters. "Anything for you?" Lena asks, taking her packet of newspaper, throwaways, and a bill. " 'Fraid not," Nell replies with a lilt. How cheerful her guile. Did this happen?

Home over Christmas, Nell is in the barn mucking out, making the best of it as Lena does when sawdust and manure freeze overnight. Everyone looks moth-eaten. Camels are handsomer. And there she is grooming the horses in spring. Handfuls of their shedding fur fly up into the breeze. The birds will take tufts of it for their nests. Lena begins to remember the two daughters at Richard's funeral, one on either side in the university chapel; then she stubbornly puts this frame away—not to be revisited until safe. Memory glosses over, invents, modifies. Surely there were quarrels, fits of depression. Pots spilled. Toilets backed up. The daughters are there; they glow.

It is morning of the second day. All over town backyard ponies are being curried and combed. Burdocks are picked out of their tails. Candy-box ribbons are braided in their manes and bacon fat is rubbed on their hooves to make them shine. Children, awake far too early, are putting on costumes that will fall into tatters before the day is over. At least fourteen local farmers are polishing their oxen for the pulling contest. A dozen others, preparing for the annual chopping exhibition, are honing their axes and splitting mauls. Simple Ben, who is said to have lost most of his wits in the last Great War and ever after has ridden his bicycle up and down Route 27, rain or shine, is putting on the top half of an old Air Force uniform. He strokes the cap, especially the visor. Today he will cover the route of the parade a dozen times.

The banner bearing HEALTH, HEAD, HEART, HANDS, the 4-H insignia, is being freshly ironed in the Milzcuiski kitchen. In Portland, the Shriners Marching Band, complete with purple fezzes, clambers aboard a rented bus for the trip to Ramawa. On the Ramawa green, three workmen with wrenches tighten the pipe connections for the Ferris wheel. Vendors' stands are being set up in a fairly orderly fashion. There will be some jockeying for better places later on.

On Lena's hill, Evvie is still sleeping. Even on her Lady Godiva day, sleep holds Evvie fast. She will drift in its grip until Lena raps her awake. Joshua, who has been up for hours, is trying to eat breakfast. Lena worries that nothing will stay down if she bullies him. He swallows some milk. Two bites of toast. Later, Lena consoles herself, there will be quick energy from cotton candy.

All too soon after the parade begins, Lena reaches the point of restlessness. She foresees a picture of the Ramawa Fall Foliage Festival shining forth from the Portland Sunday rotogravure. Everyone quaint in town—Ben on his bicycle, Herman Haverness atop the antique fire pumper, Lila Baines gotten up as a belly dancer perched on her white Arabian stallion—is fixed in time by the glossy taint of too-bright colors bleeding into one another. The drum majorettes are a sickly pink. On the Betsy Ross float the basting seams of the costumes rip open to expose dungarees and tee shirts, a ragbag of red, white, and blue.

Only Joshua is in harmony. Astride one of the matched oxen pulling Evvie's mother's prize-winning float, a covered wagon built onto a flatbed tagalong, Joshua frowns importantly into the sun. His bleached flour-sack tunic and his shock of blond hair intensify the rich brown of the animals' burnished coats. Joshua is going west in triumph.

Four of Nell's letters from Kampala also move west on this day. From Dakar they catch an Air France flight to New York. Tomorrow or the next day they will come by mail truck from Portland to the postmistress's cage in the general store downtown. Evvie's father, who inquires secretly every morning on his way to the piano factory, will personally bring the letters up the hill.

Lena goes out the door to deal with Marigold. Jeeper excretes on the front lawn. News of Nell, only eight days old, makes its bright way west.

Why Can't
We Live Together Like
Civilized Human Beings?

Remember Humphrey Bogart in his greatest role? Remember the lead-in voice? A tortuous, roundabout refugee trail—Paris to Marseilles, across the Mediterranean to Oran, then across the rim of Africa to Casablanca in French Morocco. . . . I was an adolescent then, completely under the spell of Bogey and Bergman, Lorre and Greenstreet. Now the world runs faster; nowhere can you see a broader cross-section of it than in airports. Heathrow, Zurich, Athens, Frankfurt. Caste marks on caramel foreheads, diamonds in nostrils, turbans, djellebas, chadors, double-knits, and tribal scars, all crammed into the space, say, of a football stadium.

Downstairs on Pier B in the Frankfurt Airport, travelers depart for Sofia, Varna, Djivdiv, and Odessa. Public-address messages are delivered in one language only. Other communications—a zap with the metal-detector ring, a once-over body pat—are conducted by gesture. A jerk of the chin if you pass. If not, it's behind the curtain and strip to your underwear.

No telescoping jetways down here. Restive, I people-watch, assign nationalities and life histories to the thirty-odd comrades who wait with me for the bus that goes out to the plane to Djivdiv. Not one could be taken for American. And there are none of those volatile Germans and other Westerners who roam around upstairs in blue jeans and slogan-bedecked tee shirts, carrying hit records in bull's-eye plastic bags or pyramiding junk food on Styrofoam trays. Littering, American style, as they go. Down here, the tone is somber, dress tacky.

I can't help watching it all go past. It's my training, my profession, to see documentaries in anthills. In the perilous days of the blacklist I put together my first film. Cruising Sunset Strip I interviewed Miss Cornflakes beauties in Walgreen's and bit players on the make in the courtyard of the Marmont. McCarthy and his colleagues took the Great American Dream seriously; there was nothing subversive about easy success.

I survived that era to do a script on sandhogs followed by a grainy, deserted Alcatraz in black and white. In '64 I shot the mall by Sproul Hall at the height of the Berkeley turmoil: Mario Savio on top of a car, his shy person-to-person stutter magically erased by the magnetism of the crowd. Joan Baez, throaty with zeal, hordes of students storming Sproul, lugging their sleeping bags and granola mixes past the white marble columns. Followed by tear gas, dogs, riot police. Hundreds going limp, bounced down the stairs. *Newsweek* bought three of my stills.

A disenchanted year or so later I did a short raying out from my own daughter, Tory, a tough, lithe six-year-old hanging upside down from the school monkey bars. She was missing two front teeth. I spent weeks chasing gap-toothed kids on playgrounds and parks, asking startled but

150

gratified parents to sign release slips. It was an art piece, and it flopped. But Tory loved it. I said it was her Valentine's Day present. Her psychiatrist father, from whom I was already estranged—we said estranged back then—sent her an elaborate heart-shaped music box that played "Let Me Call You Sweetheart" when you raised the lid. He said he had to buy it for her then or never, between her Oedipal phase and her latency period. That was the kind of backhand he played.

He hated what I did. It was voyeurism, he said; the zoom lens was a substitute for penile penetration—that sort of calculated remark. I said what he did was dilettantism. Years on the couch but no one got better. After that, we couldn't stay together. Tory lived with him weekends and every August until she was sixteen. I filled up his side of the bed with books and crackers, pillows, a heating pad. Sometimes I read all night and slept all morning. Some of my best friends were men. Two were lovers. The second moved on five years ago.

Last year my film on migrant fruit pickers won a Critics Circle Award. There was a nice little flurry over it. I suspect the notice got me invited to the film festival in this tiny Balkan nation the size of Rhode Island. The Lurgian Film Makers Union drew up a list. I suspect I was an alternate on it and squeaked by when one of the big names dropped off. Something like:

—Quick, Tolko, Hilda Haversham can't come! Get us some other woman docu-maker from the West. Radical is okay, but nobody too famous. And nothing flamboyant, no lesbians. And Tolko, try not to pick a drunk.

Tolko Rakov became my personal friend five years ago at the Cannes Festival. He must have been consulted; I mean, how else would I have been chosen?

The Lurgian Festival commemorates the death of Jagar Nikolov, their famous writer-director, who rose from humble origins in the Zlat Mountains to lead a band of partisans in the Resistance. After Lurgia staged its People's Revolution and emerged on the right side in World War II, Nikolov seized a camera. His career took off like a sidewinder.

And he *was* good. He had a sixth sense about how long to hold an establishing shot, when to crosscut, and how far. Especially how to use amateurs—in the trade we call them non-actors—to their best advantage. In the sixties while the Swedes were making tiresome crazy pornos, Nikolov retaliated by doing women. He filmed women asleep, women in childbirth. Women sweeping the streets. Women dancers, acrobats, steeplechasers. Then that knockout about a Lurgian interpreter who falls in love with her client, the mayor of some damp industrial city in the English midlands. It showed all over the West as *Ludmilla and the Lord Mayor* and made Maya Madonya a star. At first, Lurgian officials viewed its popularity with consternation. I heard later that they planned to veto its export, but something softened inside the Party and the film popped up at Cannes. The rest is history.

Just before his seventieth birthday Nikolov died. Now they want to give him their highest film award, the Bronze Bear—posthumously. Mourning over, deification sets in. Fifty of us from all over the world are going to partake in the laying on of hands. Expenses paid.

The plane, an elderly Ilyushin, is packed. I crane my neck to see if I recognize other Westerners. No luck. Unblessed by demonstrations of safety features, we taxi for takeoff. No cautionary message about your seat belt. No card in seat-back pocket; no pocket. Above my head is a little container marked in Cyrillic and English: SAFETY ROPE. IN EMERGENCY BREAK OPEN TO FIND INFORMATION ABOUT SAFETY ROPE.

How weak an American's grasp of the geography of Eastern Europe! We fly over interlocking spines of snowy mountains. I take these to extend across Yugoslavia, Rumania, Bulgaria, but in what order? I who have lived through World War II, the Suez Crisis, and the Berlin airlift, cannot say with certainty what country abuts what. Two hours and thirty minutes from Frankfurt, Djivdiv, Lurgia's single city, sticks up its mix of onion spires and skyscrapers.

At planeside a delegation from the Film Union; they whisk me off the tarmac in a Lada—a Fiat the Russians now make—deliver me into a VIP lounge I instantly recognize: It is my grandmother's living room in Atlantic City, circa 1938. Overstuffed chairs with antimacassars, Tiffany lamps, immense gilt mirrors losing their silver backs. It turns out I am the last Union guest to arrive in Djivdiv. I have already missed visiting the shooting grounds where Nikolov's younger brother was *executioned* by the Nazis. Carillons were *having play*, also a cannon.

—*Quel dommage*, I murmur, uneasy how long we are to proceed in broken English-French.

And then Tolko, now in his forties, smiling at me over his wild, see-through carrot beard. The skin around Tolko's eyes crinkles when he smiles. Tolko's forehead expands its domain as his ginger hair recedes. He has the thick, columnar, yet sinewy frame of a waltzing bear. We embrace Lurgian style: a buss to the left cheek, a buss to the right, again the left, then a clasping double shake of shoulders. It is an art form, this greeting.

—Since four years I do not see you, Tolko says. —You don't change since four years, Patricia.

—Since four years you're still making translation through French. And what a liar you are, Tolko! I've gone quite gray. Also my face is falling in.

Something like tears brim in Tolko's warm brown eyes. He wants to hug me again, but this is a public reception. We content ourselves with shoulder clasping.

By now I have been relieved of my passport and return

153

ticket; I feel stateless and naked. Where are the documents to be held?

—For safekeeping, Tolko interprets. —In a box at the Hotel Commemorat People Plaza.

I never hear Lurgia's chief hostelry referred to in any other way than by this awkward cluster of names. Among English-speaking visitors it is called the H. C. Double-P.

At dinner I meet an Indian woman in a plum-colored sari, a Canadian, and a Swede. With Tolko we are the Ingliski table. Wine flows in and around a meal heavy with pork, unidentified root vegetables, and prunes. Brandy follows. Talk ranges from Eisenstein to Fellini. The Canadian, a crew-cut six-footer with huge, chapped hands, describes the physical hardships involved in filming the Yukon from dogsled. Ice on the lens. Chilblains. Mechanical failures.

Afterwards I make a great show of having drunk too much, necessitating a turn outdoors. I have seen enough spy thrillers to know not to open personal conversation on the premises.

Once Tolko and I are out of range, I ask. —What happened to Dora? I watched all the papers but nothing was ever printed. And the child?

Tolko replies a little stiffly. —I have a new wife, Patricia. And a son. He has two years now.

—He is two years old now, I correct automatically. —But I'm so sorry!

—Please. It is water down the bridge. Far down.

Five years ago I met Tolko's wife at the Cannes Festival. For the most part Lurgian women are massive. They look square, hewn from the native iron-streaked stone. But Dora, a thin, dark, intense woman with masses of curly hair that flew about her skull as if agitated from within, put me in mind of a flamenco dancer. She had that kind of feline grace. Actually, she was a ballerina but no longer performed with the national troupe. The child, a black-eyed cherub of three or four, eerily resembled her mother and rode frequently on Tolko's shoulders. Up and down the Croisette he trotted with her, overtaking starlets who promenaded with poodles in matching fur coats, passing movie sharks in Cardin shirts and silvered-over dark glasses. Anushka, they called the little one.

I remember thinking how secure Tolko's position in the Party was for him to travel freely with his family. London, Vienna, Paris, he told me, expansive with gestures. And each year to Cannes. Each year the blue, blue Mediterranean and the beaches of pebbles the British call shingles. Tolko the word-monger added it to his collection. He was enchanted to chat up an American. Could we speak more tomorrow? And tomorrow.

Few of the Eastern bloc lingered for the inevitably sodden cocktail parties after screenings. Tolko, whose extraordinary beard rendered him highly visible, could almost always be detected across the room, glass in hand. Beside him, opposite him almost always, the wife. And at Dora's side or his, Anushka like a docile house pet being hand-fed crackers and little celery sticks.

We turn to go along the edge of a little park. The sky over Djivdiv is thick with stars.

—Take my arm, Patricia. You are dizzy from the slivovitz, we must walk to restore you.

I stagger unconvincingly in case we are being watched, and Tolko puts his arm around my waist. For support, of course. —You remember how I went that day in Nice? I was the messenger.

His wife had run off with another man; he had helped her do so. It's commonplace, running off, taking, or more usually abandoning, a child. It happens forty times a day

155

in Manhattan and Queens alone. But Tolko's wife defected. She flew out on forged papers he risked his career, perhaps even his life, to obtain. Now in Paris Anushka is Annette, a chunky eight-year-old with thick plaits. Her new father, a prosperous television executive, was once a dancer.

—The whole year I wept. I considered to kill myself. All my letters came back unopened. She did not even call for them. I who had let her go, and the child!

—How terrible for you!

—It was necessary. From the first she would have been followed, she would have been arrested and I along with her. She is a passionate woman, she does not consider the consequences.

We walk up and down, shoulder to shoulder, as if on a shuffleboard court.

—In the beginning, when she was cold to me, I begged her to tell me. Why can't we live together like civilized human beings? She was frank with me, she replied that she loved another. This man she had met in Budapest, on a tour. She begged me to divorce from her, she would find a way to go to him. Passionate Dora, she would have gone directly to prison. You see, then. I could not keep her with me against her will.

—But to lose the child, too.

—You knew she is his child, Tolko said simply. —But I loved her as my own.

I remember this and can think of no appropriate response.

—I suffered. I tortured myself about the marriage; what had I done? When she told me who was the father of Anushka it was like a death. Correction: It *was* a death. And then after she defected I was placed under surveillance. They took away my union membership for six months. I could do nothing, only instructional films, how to load a rifle, how to operate a computer, and so on. I was to be declared a parasite, but friends interceded. So I had to decide, a living death or a fresh beginning.

—And you've married again?

—Yes, I am married with a Georgian, she is from the heart of the Caucasus. Dora was an intellectual, and with a martyr's soul. How do you say this, a death wish? It was for the best, her flight. Vassela is of the soil. We have in common a love of mountains. We climb together. She is very young, she has only twenty-seven years.

—She is only twenty-seven.

—Yes. The little boy, Sasha—Alexander—is soon two. My wife is again *enceinte*. Expectant.

—Pregnant is better.

—Yes. He smiles. A metal molar glints in the street light.

—Perhaps this time it will be a girl.

—Perhaps. In the distant corner of our make-believe shuffleboard I hug him. I hold his beard, this gentle Lurgian lyricist. My comrade Tolko.

In Cannes the year Tolko and I met, Cecily Tyson was being discovered in *The Autobiography of Miss Jane Pitman*. Born in slavery, raised up through the Civil War and Reconstruction, she plays every age from adolescence to her ninetieth year. Near the end we see her reminiscing with wrinkled dignity. I didn't quite believe the old-age part, but the crowd at Cannes did. They came blinking out of the Palais des Festivals, out of the Salle Cocteau, they roamed the lobbies, bars, and mezzanines of the Majestic, the Beau Séjour, they overflowed the terraces of the Carlton, and everywhere they buzzed not about the celluloid San Francisco drug bust or the Greek partisans epic, but about Cecily Tyson. What a star! At her personal appearance, cops in riot helmets had to hold back the fans.

The contrast between indoors and out addled the

senses. In May the fields in the Alpes Maritimes shone chrome yellow with rape blossoms. Wild poppies in shades of pink, red, and orange bloomed along the edges. The willows and sycamores were in full leaf. In that painterly light, little blue tents full of film buffs had sprung up on all the Campings. Every hotel in Cannes, every hotel down the Riviera in either direction, Toulon to Cap Ferrat, was full.

The Lurgians were housed across from the railroad station in the slightly sleazy Hôtel du Commerce. It was noisy but convenient. And expensive; the state paid. During the Film Festival even the price of sleeping on muslin sheets in a second-class hostelry trebled.

I was staying with friends of friends twenty kilometers north in Saignot. My bedroom window opened on a luxuriant row of cypresses that ran downhill into the village. Plumes of smoke were pasted on the avenue of trees, as in travel posters. Each morning, Marie-Laurence, my hostess, emerged from the kitchen door and carried her coffee out to the patio table. In a moment the heavy brown smell of a Gauloise rose to my judas-perch.

Evenings in the parlor I tensed on the rim of the chair as on a diving board, ready, dreading the plunge. The conversation pumped and fell back in a medley of languages, sometimes two or three in a single mouth making a point to the others.

—Madame has not seen *La Paloma*, the Brazilian film? Now it's too late. The Spanish journalist's satisfaction was evident in any language. —You've missed it.

(Idiot. Christ came, and where were you? Bathing in the Mediterranean.)

Laure's husband, Richard, presided over this salon. I listened respectfully, a *pique-assiette*, a freeloader, one among many; always there were guests in this house. Writers, painters, *cinéastes* passing through. They sent back their new books gratefully inscribed: for Richard, without whom, et cetera.

Half American, half Swedish, Richard had been covering the Cannes Festival for a European English-language syndicate for years. Still handsome, with the profile of a falcon and the blue eyes of a Crusader, he spoke six languages and, since he did nothing lightly, was fluent in all to which he laid claim.

Of course he was writing a book. Mornings, Laure brought him his tea. At nine his typewriter started up and kept up its bright anarchic chatter in another wing of the house while we puttered from kitchen to garden and I returned to my third-floor quarters to make notes on yesterday's events "downtown." "Downtown" had become Richard's and my American name for the jazzy resort on the Riviera. I was doing an article to be called "Making a Meal out of Cannes"; it appeared in the Sunday magazine section of the *New York Times.*

The Lurgian booth at the festival, wedged between the Czechs and the Hungarians, both of whom had sizable delegations, occupied an alcove at the end of the corridor. It appeared to have been partitioned off as an afterthought. The plasterboard walls enclosing the man with the carrot beard, the flamenco dancer, and the swarthy, round-eyed child were handsomely decorated with a montage of horse pictures. These magnetized me each time I passed on my way to the *toilettes des dames.* I nodded and smiled on my round trips. One day, browsing from booth to booth with Richard—who knew everyone—I stopped to ask about the horses.

Richard had met Tolko earlier, once in Hungary and once in Greece, before the troubles. He introduced us and we began *en français*, but Tolko's English was a cut above my French and I was happy to switch. —These are Arabic horses from the state farm in Plornitz. You are familiar?

159

He showed me on a map. —Here, on the eastern slopes of the Zlats. Yes, Arabics of the Polish bloodline. They all descend from the famous stallion Gasphar.

In between talk of line-breeding and out-crosses, Tolko's life story emerged. His father had worked a small farm south of the Zlats where the family raised pigs and apples and grew vegetables for market on the narrow but fertile plateau that bisects Lurgia. Every time Tolko brought up his peasant childhood, he appeared transfigured. He was haloed in his golden past: the little wood and plaster dwelling with a pump in the front yard, a privy in the back. The pear trees, their white blossoms. The plowhorse named Katja, so kind, so patient. His own shaggy pony, a biter. The scar on his left arm from one such bite.

—Of course now it is a better life. The farms are collectivized, with indoor toilets and running water. Many with electricity. A better diet for all.

Still, he rhapsodized over the hardships. The snows of winter, the flies of summer. His longing to return to the soil, to have again a little place in the country. Yes, when he fulfilled his quota of films, he would return to dig in the earth, to cultivate a garden. To curry again a horse.

From the beginning it was easy to be a friend of Tolko Rakov. He had what Margaret Mead once called the gift of perfect presence—the ability to make any number of people from any assortment of backgrounds feel honored, amused, at home with one another. From him I began to understand something about myself: No matter how vigorously I complained about American foreign policy or excoriated domestic infighting, it was affectionate criticism. Tolko might satirize his small-nationhood, mock the Soviet hierarchy, and sigh his desire to live as decadently as in the West, but he too was a patriot.

—You farmers, Richard called us. —You toilers of the furrow, sniffing up every clod. All that sweat and instinct.

He sighed and signaled the barman while Tolko and I

160

traded anecdotes about animals.

—You know of course that the horse collar was a Lurgian discovery, Tolko told us. —Previously—Richard, pay attention to this fact, it has immense social importance—previously men plowed with oxen. These oxen were yoked to push by the forehead. He demonstrated this, pressing his fists against his hairline, lowering his head to surge forward. —It was not a useful method for horses. The first drawings of horse collars are found scratched on Lurgian water jugs in the sixth century.

—So, plowing with horses meant better crops? I asked.

—Yes, and better nutritions gave the first leisure time. Without leisure there can be no art.

Richard waved his wineglass to take in the crescent of aquamarine Mediterranean. —And so the entire Cannes Festival can be blamed on the Lurgian horse collar.

—Exactly.

Lurgian was not one of Richard's languages. Tolko did not interest him; he was not, *au fond*, an intellectual. —It's that Slavic temperament. They're all so Dostoevskian, all thinking with their stomachs. He had contempt for their film technique. —Everything in reds and greens. Christ! It's a regular Valentine's Day–Christmas package, so simplistic. You have to go north, where the blood thins and the long nights turn people inward; that's where art begins.

—Oh? What about all those painters trooping down here? What about the restorative powers of the South of France?

He thought for a minute. —It's okay for the British. For northern types in general. They have the discipline to withstand it. Not good for Americans. Terrible for the Soviets and their satellites.

I had been reading the account of Aldous Huxley's life with Maria at Sanary, near Toulon. Sitting al fresco at the Carlton with my campari and soda while photographers elbowed past to get intimate poses of the sequinned *vedettes,* I thought about a documentary: I called it the Festival of Contrasts.

In my documentary it is 1930. Aldous comes to breakfast looking sleepy. It is 10 A.M., the mail has not yet come. Maria has been up for hours working in her garden, spraying her artichokes. Breakfast is served by the quiet and respectful family retainer, whose only character flaw is a craving for chocolates. Aldous retires to work. At noon everybody troops to the sea to bathe. Afterwards, the midday repast, fruit and cheeses and chilled wines. All the mechanics of the household flow smoothly, gently, eternally onward. Ardent and sympathetic friends come to call, there are uninterrupted work periods to think, read, write. When the sun sets, a stroll or another swim, a quiet hour alone for the couple in their upstairs rooms to refresh and dress for dinner, then descend immaculate in their fresh-laundered white trousers and thin Egyptian-cotton shirts. After dinner, a contemplative time in the garden with Beethoven on the gramophone, the scent of lime trees and wetted earth. No mosquitoes sully this idyll. No writer's block, no difficult menstrual periods, no tantrums brought on by boredom or ideological differences.

In my fantasy documentary I contrast this idyll with shots of Bergman and Bogdanovich. Bo Widerberg with a small child harnessed to his chest. Male and female prostitutes and a transvestite good-naturedly working up clients at the same downtown intersection. I end on frames from a somewhat overwrought short of Tolko's in which native Lurgian dancers risk their lives with fire and swords. Richard is right; it is largely done in red and green.

It was a relief to come back to Saignot at night, even though it meant risking my life in the rented Renault Cinq on the tortuous mountain roads. —*Il faut faire klaxonner, klaxonner,* Laure advised me. Oncoming cars never lowered their beams. Bluffing, they rushed past as I wilted and squeezed as close to the edge as I dared.

Richard, after his room-temperature scotch and seltzer, faded like the Cheshire cat. From time to time machine-gun bursts from his typewriter abovestairs. Once or twice I caught sight of him through the french doors of the disheveled dining room where Laure and I clumsily formulated our conversations. He crunched gravel underfoot on the terrace, his shadow passed the window, he was gone. We sipped *eau de vie*—for me it is what the name says, said Laure, the water of life—and played some hands of gin. Richard was going up to Vence to review the Giacomettis. We decided to go with him and make it an overnight. Their Jaguar stood in the courtyard on blocks awaiting the return of the only mechanic in Saignot who could be trusted with it. We would go in the Renault.

False Arrest, a British imitation of Antonioni's *Blow-Up*, was screened the next morning in the Salle Cocteau. Afterwards I ran into Tolko lighting up a little black cigarette and squinting into the noon glare. We eavesdropped together as other filmgoers trickled past. I made mental note of a few more cinema clichés for my article: —Did you notice how the color yellow is chemically involved in the scene? —Yes, he is quintessentially a societal director.

We wandered down the rue d'Antibes for a coffee.

—Where's your family today?

He made a face. —Shopping.

—Ah, falling prey to decadent capitalism.

Tolko gave me one of his radiant smiles. —In Lurgia the Russian joke is very much in vogue. "Tell me, if capitalism is hurling itself over the precipice, why are we hurrying to catch up with it?"

—Why, indeed?

—Perhaps for nostalgia. My father and I in a little *cabine* by the sea, we make wine together every autumn. He has only two hectares but the grapes are thick there, and we do them together every year. More than we can use. We give many liters away. When my father dies I should like to have a son to teach the old method.

—Why a son? Why not a daughter? That's very sexist, Tolko, for a good socialist.

—She is not my child. I love her like my own but she will not stay, Patricia.

I was astonished to see tears standing in his eyes.
—Something's wrong, isn't it? Something's terribly . . . can I help?

Tolko scraped back his chair. —Not here.

We circled Cannes while he told me. The money for the false documents was waiting in Nice. A package at the post office, General Delivery. Yes, it was dangerous but not impossible. The French forgeries were of the highest quality. He and his wife were both Party members in good standing. Dora had always been very discreet. He thought it quite likely that she was above suspicion.

—Come with us to Vence tomorrow. It isn't far, you can take the car and go on to Nice in an afternoon. Can you drive a shift car?

—It is what you call four-on-the-floor?

—Tolko, you amaze me. Where did you learn that?

—From Hollywood, Patricia.

—Of course.

—We'll stay at the Fondation one night and drive back here the following morning. If you like, we can say that Richard wanted to interview you for his syndicate.

—*Bon. Enfin.* We shook hands. He mustered a smile, full face in the sun. The metal in his back tooth gleamed.

We left the next day, after the morning screening. Richard drove, Laure beside him. Tolko and I sat scissored in the little back seat. It was impossible not to touch shoulders and knees. The day was perfectly clear, the sun fierce, the sea a pale green. When we arrived in Vence, I went over the Michelin map with Tolko, showed him the registration in the glove compartment. We waved him off, watching as he crept cautiously around the town square and turned onto the direct route to Nice.

It seemed safer not to discuss Tolko's mission with Laure and Richard. I said merely that he had some errands to run, including getting new frames for his glasses. This part was true. Of that trip I remember the cherries we ate, picking them from overhanging boughs as we strolled through the Fondation's grounds. I remember the Giacomettis, strange, attenuated, drip-castled creatures, and I remember the decrepit little cabins of the artist colony in which a heterogenous collection of talents worked, fought, formed alliances, and staged their suicide attempts.

Tolko was terribly withdrawn on the drive back to Cannes. I took his hand and squeezed it intermittently; I suppose I hoped I was giving him courage. It was a lovely hand with strong, square fingers. Fine ginger hairs decorated his forearms. Richard stopped at a chemist's and bought Tolko a headache powder, the kind French druggists fold up in a triangular slip of paper for you to sprinkle into your mineral water. At the Hôtel du Commerce he made a grave and proper adieu, promised he would write, and vanished into the lobby. I did not see him again, although I stayed on until the Yugoslavs and Czechs dismantled their exhibits. The Lurgian booth had disappeared overnight. Richard sleuthed around for me but turned up nothing. I didn't press the matter—I sensed Tolko was in enough trouble already. A news story by someone like Richard could only make things worse.

Now we are leaving Djivdiv on two Mercedes buses, four dozen film-makers from twenty countries. Everyone is wearing a camera, Satiyah of the sari, two.

—Of course, shoot! says Molenko, the Deputy Minister for Cultural Affairs, from the front of the bus. —The People's Republic invites you to take pictures as you wish.

165

Djivdiv hurtles past, a city of blocky stone buildings and open parks with little ponds full of ducks. I spot a lame horse being dragged at a trot behind a cart drawn by an only somewhat sounder dray. The creature hitched behind is truly traveling on three legs. If they are fetching him to the butcher, couldn't they go more slowly? I aim, but Tolko's hand is over the lens.

—Please.

—He said anything we wished.

—Of course. But couldn't you wait for the starving children and perhaps some lepers?

I put down my Minolta.

In about ten kilometers the superhighway ends abruptly. We swing onto a winding country road and begin the gradual ascent into the Zlats. The spectacle is awesome, the hairpin turns—there are no guard rails—alarming. In Slito, a sleepy provincial city Chekhov is said to have visited, we have a thirty-minute rest stop, long enough to check into the one hotel that serves the region. Higher in the Zlats, only occasional guesthouses are available. We will return here this evening.

In the days when Laramie, Wyoming was still a territory, hotels looked like this one. I know it well; it is a Western stage set. Each room has a washbasin and a rudimentary shower which looms out of the ceiling and aims at a hole in the floor. The *tooaletti*, it develops, are at the end of the corridor. Tolko and I are assigned rooms next to each other and receive our keys. These are massive affairs, too big to put in a pocket.

In precisely thirty minutes we are under way again.

—You see how smoothly the schedule runs in a socialist state, Tolko says, perhaps to indicate he has forgiven me for the horse. Now we have a police escort to protect us against oncoming traffic. Or is it the other way around? The climb is precipitous, the view breathtaking. Where there are clearings, flocks of sheep cling to the steep hillsides. Elsewhere, pine, spruce, birch, and larch, densely packed. Here a few donkeys, a workhorse or two. Terraced plantings, fences and stockades intricately laced from saplings.

—How do you call these in English?

I search for the word, a long rummage. —Wattles.

We pass an outdoor market. I look back longingly at the jumble of items for barter.

Jagar Nikolov's birthplace: Zlatia, 35 kilometers above Slito, altitude, 2,100 meters. Nothing I have read or seen has prepared me for our triumphal procession into the village. The cobbled streets are lined with children in their gymnasium costumes. Some wave red flags, others hold out flowers. Women in traditional native dress—ornately embroidered blouses, felt skirts, scarves and sashes—push toward us with pewter tankards of hot wine and platters of round bread. Tolko demonstrates: You tear off a piece of bread and dip it in the colored salt grains. Soldiers, all with red armbands, the men of the village in elaborate and bright folk dress. I think suddenly of Richard; red and green predominate.

We progress slowly, as through a funnel, into the village square, accepting flowers, mouthfuls of the sweet mulled wine, against a backdrop of folk songs, piccolo, and drum. Host families press toward us, for we are to be parceled out to individual homes for the midday meal. Tolko and I and Satiyah, resplendent but chilled in her gauzy gold sari, enter the modest home of the village councilman.

The meal opens with at least a score of toasts to health, to international friendship, to the film festival, the film industry, the People's Republic, the health of our leaders and generations to come. Slivovitz loosens all tongues. We are awash in feelings of love of fellowman. Romantic love of humankind. Of the animal kingdom. *Pa drotchka!* the toast goes round, followed by clinking glasses, the crossing of arms. And to Jagar Nikolov, to his sacred memory, many a raised glass.

On the way to the town square for the outdoor memorial services, I say to Tolko, —It's the new Christianity, this cult of Nikolov. What we just had are the good-little-infant-Jesus stories. And some Jesus-the-regular-guy stories.

Tolko glances casually around, but I think he is checking to see if we abut any English speakers. —Nothing about his two wives and twelve mistresses. In his last years he showed a preference for young boys.

I pretend to be shocked. —Sacrilege!

—It is well known. But of course here in Lurgia homosexuality is not a problem.

—Really?

—Really. Tolko is very dry. —It is against the law.

None of the speeches is short. —The smaller the nation the longer its official remarks, Tolko whispers. Supposedly he stands close to me so he can interpret. Mostly he says et cetera et cetera et cetera, like Yul Brynner, but he does render word for word the flamboyant parts about protecting Lurgian maidens from the Ottomans for five centuries and in recent times guarding them from the fascists.

Dusk is falling. From where we stand we can actually see daylight shrink up the mountain face until finally only the white peaks are visible. Young men carrying flaming torches come single file into the square, followed by two bands playing the Lurgian national anthem, very dirge-like and stirring, and still another children's choir. The little ones are dressed flimsily in shorts and high socks. They are a study in red knees and composure, and the sweetness of their voices brings tears to my eyes.

The songs they are given to sing allude to certain bloody moments in history. Tolko gives me the full treatment.

—In battle against the Ottomans a Lurgian army was brought to its knees. This was the tenth century of the

168

common era. The captain of the conquering army ordered the eyes of every nine Lurgian soldiers in a row to be gouged out. One eye in every tenth face was to be spared. In this way the defeated army could be led back in disgrace by its own men.

—So that's the root meaning of the word decimate! Tolko, do you know what an ottoman is, in English? It's a hassock, something you put your feet on.

—Wishful Lurgian revenge.

Everywhere we are told about the Ottoman oppression. The twin teardrop-shaped lakes above Zlatia are named for a local maiden who saved her family from slaughter by agreeing to enter the Ottoman harem. But moments before she rode off with the conqueror she gouged out her eyes. Et cetera et cetera et cetera. Gouging is relished. No Lurgian folk tale is complete without one—as no John Ford Western is complete without a lynching.

Only when it is fully dark does the ceremony conclude. We adjourn to the town hall, so newly constructed that the bathroom fixtures have not yet been provided with plumbing, a problem the men solve casually behind the yew trees and the women by a brisk walk across the square to the local tavern. We are to eat again, drink again, dance. I am seized by a burly national and carried off in something like a schottische. Ten minutes later I return to Tolko's side breathless and quite drunk on my partner's fumes. The only way to survive this evening, clearly, is to enter into it. Between dances I guzzle *minerali* and a little vodka. Moderation, I caution my thirst, elated to think I am still sober. I do not take into account the altitude.

At midnight we are ushered aboard our buses for the trip down to Slito. Despite hairpin turns, little of that ride comes back to me. I remember trudging upstairs in the hotel, I remember Tolko's admonition to lock my door from the inside. I stumble through undressing and collapse into the lumpy, narrow bed. I shiver under my eiderdown; it is impossible to grow warm enough to sleep.

Two hours later I come bolt upright, aware that everything I ate and drank is about to reverse. Frantic, I struggle with the key. It turns but will not click the lock. There is the hole in the floor for the shower—too narrow. The washbasin? Terrible. Cold, frightened, sick, I knock on the wall of Tolko's room, but even in my desperation I don't knock loudly. I don't want to arouse the whole hotel. I can hear him snoring gently, rhythmically, like a small sea rising and falling. But how to tell him? I push open the casement window, see a two-foot-wide ledge and climb out on it in my pale blue nylon travel robe with the white piping bought for the occasion, and in two steps am rapping on Tolko's window. He bursts from the bed in his white undershorts, looks wildly once around the room, and rushes to lift me in. He says several things in Lurgian, never translated.

—My key doesn't work. I'm going to throw up.

Practical man, he yanks on his trousers, unfastens the door, and speeds me down the hall, where I retch as quietly as possible in the unisex *tooaletta*. Barefoot, Tolko holds my head. Bare-chested in his room, Tolko washes my face. The icy water shocks me free of nausea. He tucks me tenderly into his bed. We have left the window open; a glacial wind from the Zlats pervades the room. Tolko pulls on a sweater, climbs into the little bed beside me, and folds me in a comradely embrace against his chest.

In the morning we discuss how to effect the transition. Tolko wants to take the window route, fetch the defective key from the lock, return to this room, go out in the hall, and attempt to unlock my door from the outside. I protest; it is my key, my room, my window. I will go back the way I came. I tighten the sash on my travel robe and step out through the window once more. After I am dressed I slip the key under the door to Tolko, who does indeed unlock it from outside.

Satiyah has just flung open the musty purple draperies to inspect the mountains. As she cranes her neck for a view of the revered Norndska Flume, I emerge through Tolko's window, pop into her line of sight, and slink along the ledge. In the corridor she lets me know this.

I begin to protest, then reconsider. Satiyah is pinched and blue with the cold. —Such things happen. You'll be discreet?

—Of course.

—It's the American way, you know. And wouldn't you like to borrow my ski sweater? You could put it on under the sari.

I go back to fetch it, through the unlocked-forever door.

—Oh, thank you, Patricia.

Having spent the long Arctic night nestled together, Tolko and I have arrived at a comfortable empathy. My head throbs with a pulse all its own. He fixes me a Lurgian-style Alka - Seltzer. Around us in the hotel, restaurant tables are half empty.

—You see, Patricia. Slito this morning is filled with hanged-overs. I congratulate you on being present at breakfast.

—Is that what this is? I thought it was my execution.

The tea comes in immense quilt-swaddled thermoses. Lacking soda crackers, I nibble a hard-boiled egg. The other choices are pickles and several kinds of salamis.

Tolko has an appropriate Russian joke. —"Interviewer: Tell me, are you making any headway in your fight against alchoholism? Subject: Oh, yes. We have already abolished breakfast."

Blessedly, our schedules are free until midafternoon. On the theory that fresh air most rapidly dispatches alcohol from the bloodstream, we set out to hike into the first ring of hills. Mahomet Lami-lami, a small wiry man stylishly outfitted in ski costume, leads. Satiyah, snug now in an ancient sheepskin coat the desk clerk has loaned her, follows. Tolko and I, sweatered and scarfed, stamp along behind. Lami-lami speaks only French and Syrian, Satiyah, Hindi and English. We skate among our various languages for a while, reviewing the tributes to Nikolov.

—They always address the dead man directly, Satiyah observes. —"Nikolov, your films are roses covering the ugly scars of the struggle for socialism," that sort of thing. It is banal, don't you think?

—It's the vocative case, I say, trying to be helpful.

Tolko reproduced both these inanities in French.

—*Ça n'existe pas en mon pays*, Lami-lami declares. —*Nous sommes en plein de sécheresse culturelle.*

—Christ! I say. —We are all fifty of us at cross-purposes.

In a little while Satiyah and Lami-lami turn off to explore the caves in which Nikolov and others spent the long winter of the fascist occupation. These are now national shrines; guides are available in five languages.

Tolko and I continue to climb toward the teardrop lakes. He takes my hand over fallen rocks and across an icy patch. And then we walk with our arms laced round each other's backs, war-weary old comrades.

—What will you do now? I mean after the festival and the public addresses?

He shrugs. —You know of course they will not again allow me to leave the country. If they permit me to keep my place in the Union, to keep my place behind the camera, *ça suffit*. I am content. I have a good family life, I am a happy husband. Who knows? Perhaps I will do Nikolov in reverse. Perhaps I will begin to write poems.

—So you are under house arrest?

—If you like. But you must understand, Patricia. I do not have the Western ambition, the *élan*, if you like. Here I am, how do you say, a big fish in a little poodle.

—Puddle.

—Yes. The other is a dog. My English is slipping since four years. For that I am sorry.

—Oh, Tolko, another four years of socialism and you won't be able to speak to a capitalist at all!

He stops on the path and turns me so we are facing each other. —*N'importe.* We will speak in French, then.

—*"Ou se trouve les toilettes?" Comme ça?*

We embrace. Tolko's beard is fragrant of cloves and cinnamon. I am overwhelmed by nostalgia and lust. We cling to each other in a kind of desperation, kissing and tasting.

Djivdiv again, a surfeit of banquets and official speeches. Two-hour harangues fall like rain on native-born and visitor alike. I learn to imitate my colleagues from the Eastern bloc: Lean on one elbow, hand propping the chin, slip away into a meditative doze, regain consciousness unobtrusively just as the speaker winds down.

Troops meanwhile are massing on various borders. Hostages taken in Iran, threats conveyed. Diplomatic pouches carry messages of near-panic back and forth. The daily Lurgian *Truth-Teller (Protchka-Pitschka)* excoriates the United States with rising rhetoric. I flinch as Tolko makes the dry line-by-line translation. —"Imperialist, reactionary, and hegemonist circles intentionally escalate tensions in the Persian Gulf hoping to provoke a situation in which they can interfere forcefully in the internal affairs of these progressive and democratic peoples' republics."

—Do you believe this?

He counters. —Do you believe in original sin?

—I don't know what I believe, Tolko. I believe in the infinite depravity of man.

—I also. And in the socialist dream.

We are both right. In Lurgia, although housing is shabby, there is no visible ravage of the kind I have stumbled over in every industrial nation in the West. No cripples. No beggars, no drunks, no crazies. Are they put away in re-

173

education camps? No slums, no graffiti. No litter. Perhaps, like homosexuality, it is not permitted.

—But the rights of the individual, I begin.

—My grandfather, for the warmth, slept above the pigs. In winter there was only the field of turnips to eat.

—Yes, yes. I concede all this. —It is simply not the point.

—The first right is not to be hungry.

Amelioration, escalation, confrontation. The MX missile, the neutron bomb. This is how we pass our time in Djivdiv, city of trams and wooden-wheeled carts, of Mercedes buses and lame horses. *Je t'aime*, we say, in the wistful final hours.

Leaving Lurgia is both easier and harder than I anticipated. At the airport Tolko and I are again ushered into the living room of my grandmother. We share the VIP lounge with a Spanish film director whose interpreter is unaccountably missing, causing this volatile man great anguish. He has no Lurgian, no English, and only six words of French.

—*Kennst Deutsch?* Tolko, ever resourceful, asks. He is brimming to be of use, but no.

Manuel fidgets, taps his watch, asks like a bereaved child for Karli, his interpreter. And then magically, out of breath, Karli appears. All is staccato Spanish, tears, bear hugs. Manuel is escorted to his plane in bilingual dignity.

Meanwhile, Mrs. Officious Hospitality Lady has not yet appeared with my passport and tickets. The moments are fleeting. Tolko is supremely confident the system cannot break down. Two minutes past departure time the doors open, Mrs. Hospitality Lady bursts through. Her corsage of roses quivers. We rush into the car and zoom onto the tarmac. My plane's doors are closed, the engines are turning. The stairs are still in place.

—Run, Patricia! *Dépêche-toi!* Up the steps and bang on the door!

—My ticket! My passport! My baggage check!

The first two are fumbled for and produced by a now-shaken Hospitality Lady. As for the baggage check, I am on my own.

Goodbye, Tolko. War is coming. We will not meet again. I believe in the theory of socialism and in the infinite depravity of man. I believe in love and in the bicameral mind. For all these reasons we cannot live together like civilized human beings.